Sign up for our newsletter to hear
about new and upcoming releases.

www.ylva-publishing.com

Times
OF OUR LIVES

JANE WATERTON

Dedication

For Pip...
Because you said "write it," and never
stopped believing I could.
This is for you, with all my love.

Acknowledgement

I have an incredible group of people that believe in me. "Thank you" doesn't begin to express my unending gratitude for your generosity, wisdom and kindness.

To Astrid and the amazing team at Ylva Publishing for turning my dream into reality. I am so lucky to have found such a wonderful literary home.

To Erin Saluta; for your patience, guidance and encouragement with this brand-new author and for teaching me everything I didn't know.

To my family and friends all over the world; for the laughs, suggestions, encouragement and love. I am truly honoured!

Chapter 1

WINTER

"Damn, blast and bloody hell!"

Allie Richards walked down the corridor of her best friend Meg Sullivan's cottage and leant against the bedroom doorframe, surveying the large, sunlit room which currently resembled the site of a small cyclone. Clothes, magazines and newspapers tumbled from chairs and covered the floor.

"Meg, what on earth are you doing?" Allie asked, looking at the mess strewn from one end of the room to the other. "Surely it's too early for spring cleaning!"

"I'm looking for something, or at least I was when I started this process," Meg grumbled as she swept her hand through her hair. She slumped unceremoniously on the bed, causing a mini avalanche of magazines to cascade to the floor. "Now all I've done is make a huge mess and…oh, it doesn't matter," she muttered, kicking at the magazines.

Moving aside a pile of clothes, Allie sat on the bed and put her hand on Meg's arm.

"Meg, what's wrong? You have been out of sorts for months, and I'm really starting to worry about you."

"Nonsense, I'm perfectly fine," Meg said, sitting up straight.

Allie shook her head, crossing her arms. "No, it's not nonsense. It's as if you're only half here. You're not eating properly, you've started sleeping in the middle of the day, and I haven't heard you make a sarcastic remark for ages. Something's bothering you, and as your oldest friend I think I have a right to know what it is."

Meg rose from the bed and started to tidy up the room.

"Honestly, Allie," she snapped, "I'm just a little tired. There's no need to make a song and dance over it. Besides, I thought you said I needed to be less sarcastic and more... what was the word? Oh yes, *empathetic*." Meg rolled her eyes. "Now you're complaining. Sometimes I swear you are never satisfied."

Allie studied her closely. After more than forty years of friendship, she knew that no amount of pushing could get Meg to talk about anything until she was ready.

"All right," she said, raising her hands in surrender. "If you say so, I shall believe you."

Meg nodded. "Thank you. So, now that we have that out of the way, what brings you to my inner sanctum? Please tell me it's to whisk the two of us off to one of your delicious lunches and a bottle of wine."

"Well, actually I'm here to see if you're up for a game of golf? The links are free for two hours and if you need any more persuasion, I believe that Helen has gone into town for the afternoon, so we'll have the course to ourselves without any interruptions."

"Well, praise the Lord and grab the clubs," Meg said with relish. "Imagine being able to play a game of golf without dear Helen offering her totally inappropriate advice! Sounds like an opportunity too good to miss. We should call in and see if Bella and Pat are up for a foursome. Why don't we incorporate both ideas and all go out for dinner tonight as well?"

Allie frowned. "Well, I'm not sure about them. Bella wasn't feeling too well this morning, and I think she and Pat are having a quiet day."

Meg huffed, waving her hand dismissively. "Honestly, a game of golf and a night out would do Pat good. I know Bella's not well, but Pat can't look after her twenty-four hours a day. She needs time to herself as well.

Allie raised an eyebrow. "Meg, you know…"

"Oh all right, I know. I just think that Pat needs to get out more." Before Allie could reply, Meg pushed on, "Oh, let's not argue about it. The day's a-wasting. Now, I just need to find my clubs and glasses."

"Your glasses are on top of your head, and your clubs are in the hall stand."

Allie watched with a smile, as Meg touched up her lipstick and ran a comb through her short hair. Even now in her late sixties, Meg's striking looks had not diminished. Her tall, svelte body was a direct result of personal pride and a regular exercise regime.

"Lord, looks like another visit to the hairdresser next week," Meg muttered, staring critically at her reflection. "I swear these grey hairs are conspiring to make me look old. Why couldn't I have been blonde like you? No-one notices if you go grey."

Allie grinned. "I always wanted to be tall and gorgeous with long, straight, black hair and instead, here I am. Why is it that we are never satisfied with our lot?"

"Damned if I know, but I guess that's what makes life interesting. And just for the record, you are gorgeous," Meg added, giving Allie a quick kiss on the cheek.

Taking advantage of Allie's surprise, Meg shepherded her into the hallway, closing the bedroom door and picking up her keys from the sideboard. "Well, let's go. I'll sort that mess out when we get back."

Meg began to close the front door, but Allie caught her arm. "Don't forget your clubs."

As Meg turned to reply, she suddenly paled and slumped against her friend.

"Meg, are you alright? What's wrong?" Allie asked, tightening her grip. She could feel the slightest of tremors as a look of panic flashed across Meg's face.

"Sorry, yes, I'm fine." Meg blinked and took a couple of deep breaths, shaking her arm from under Allie's hand.

"Are you sure? I think you need to go and lie down…"

Meg straightened to look at Allie directly. "I said I'm fine. Just one of those silly dizzy attacks. For heaven's sake, stop fussing."

Taking another deep breath, she let herself back into the cottage and grabbed the clubs from the hall stand, then closed the door firmly and marched past Allie and down the path without another word.

Bewildered, Allie stood for a moment watching her storm off before collecting her clubs and following.

———⊰⊱———

At the clubhouse, Allie looked over the beautifully tended nine-hole course and thought again how lucky she was to be here. She still remembered the morning, six years ago, when Meg had rung her, full of enthusiasm after reading an article about OWL's Haven, a lesbian retirement home situated in

Berry on the NSW South Coast, insisting they drive down and see it.

"So, which of us is teeing off first?" Meg asked as they walked towards the first hole.

"Oh, you can. I'm happy to just potter along behind you," Allie said lazily, enjoying the feel of the sun on her back as she watched the birds skim the grass looking for insects.

Meg addressed the small white ball. Gripping her club, she raised it for the swing, then brought it down to connect perfectly.

Both women watched as it arced towards the fairway, landing just to the right of the sand trap.

"Great shot, Meg."

Allie carefully placed her ball on the tee, concentrating on the distant flag in the vain hope that her vision might somehow communicate itself to the ball. She swung her club and it hit with a resounding *whack*! Unlike Meg's, her ball veered sharply and went into the rough. She had only started playing golf recently, as a way of getting more exercise, but Meg had quickly recognised and begun coaching her natural talent.

"Damn," said Allie crossly. "I'm still pulling to the right."

Meg shook her head. "Your stance is still not quite right and it's putting you off balance as you strike the ball."

The two women started to walk to the fairway, pulling their clubs behind them. Despite Meg's dizzy turn, she had elected not to take a golf cart, preferring the exercise. A pair of kangaroos stood and watched them approach, their ears flicking, alert to danger. Deciding that the women meant them no harm, they continued grazing.

"What a glorious day!" Allie exclaimed, walking briskly to keep up with Meg's long strides. "Days like this, it feels good just to be alive. I am so glad you talked me into moving here."

"Well, break into song and I may have to kill you. I don't think I could stand a game accompanied by a Doris Day sing-along."

Allie stopped and grinned at Meg. "Glad to see you back to your normal, feisty self. I was becoming concerned."

"So glad to be able to reassure you," Meg answered drily.

"Well, you have to admit, you have been unusually quiet lately."

"I thought we'd discussed this earlier. Now are we playing golf or getting ready for a Dear Abby session?" Meg snapped.

Allie smiled. "It's your shot, I believe."

"I still can't believe I had to persuade you to move here," said Meg. "Personally, I thought it was a gift from heaven. I mean, did you honestly want to spend your days in a mixed home, with decrepit old men wherever you turned? It still gives me the shudders even thinking about it."

Allie leant on her club, watching her friend make another excellent drive. "You know I'm not as adventurous as you. I just had to give it some thought."

Meg sighed, shaking her head as they walked over to Allie's ball. "You and your thinking, Allie. It was always the same with your relationships. You'd meet someone and by the time you decided they checked all your boxes, they'd have lost interest and found someone else. Sometimes you have to just jump in and stop being so damned scared." Seeing the look of hurt on Allie's face, Meg stopped. "Oh, I'm sorry. I didn't mean to snap; it's just that, sometimes I think you miss so much by hanging back and not taking a chance. You only get one life, Allie. You've got to stop standing in the shadows and get out there."

"I know, Meg. You never get tired of telling me." Allie kicked her golf ball hard. "And just for the record, I had lots of girlfriends." At Meg's raised eyebrow, she huffed. "Alright, well, maybe not lots, but I had a few. However, never let it be said that you ever let a chance go by. At least I had a relationship that lasted longer than three weeks."

The two women glared at each other.

"Touché," Meg said quietly.

Mortified, Allie walked over to her. "I'm sorry, Meg, that was a really cheap shot." She blew out a breath. "Why are we even arguing about this? What's done is done and we're both here now, which is what's important."

Meg stared off towards the green for a moment. "Well, you've kicked your ball halfway to the green, so that's about four strokes you've conceded." Turning, she looked at Allie thoughtfully. "You know, the way you kicked that ball, maybe you should think about taking up soccer instead."

Both women started to laugh, their anger forgotten.

"Oh sure, I can just see me doing that. If someone kicked the ball towards me I'd run a mile."

Deciding to abandon their game in favour of giving Allie more practice on her swing, they went back to the driving range, where Meg dropped a ball at Allie's feet and took her through the dynamics. As Allie raised her club and twisted, Meg shook her head.

"No, that's where you're going wrong! You're twisting too far and taking the power out of your shot."

At Allie's confused look, Meg moved into position behind her. She put her arms around Allie to grab her club, settled her hips snugly into Allie's bottom from behind and pushed forward.

"Stop sticking your bottom out," Meg said. "You need to keep a straight line as you bring the club up and back down."

Holding Allie's hands over her club, she demonstrated what she meant and her hips followed Allie's into the twist. As she repeated the motion, Allie started to giggle, breaking Meg's concentration.

She pulled away and asked, "What exactly is so funny?"

Allie stopped laughing long enough to take a breath. "I'm sure it must look like we are up to something quite salacious. Anybody watching would think we are more than just good friends."

Meg considered Allie for a long moment.

"Well, we can't have that, can we?" she said lightly, turning away. "Keep practicing. It's the only way you're going to learn."

Half an hour later, after Allie's fourth successful drive, Meg applauded.

"Well done. How does that feel now?"

Allie grinned. "I think I've finally got it. You're right, it's all in the twist."

"I think that calls for a drink," Meg said.

As she packed up, Allie noticed Meg flexing her left hand.

"Getting arthritis, old girl?" she asked with a smile.

Meg stiffened. "What are you all of a sudden, my personal physician?"

Meg's tone brought Allie up short. She narrowed her eyes and stopped what she was doing. "Meg, are you going to tell me what's going on with you? First you have that attack of whatever it was this morning, and now your hand is bothering you. For heaven's sake, if something's wrong just tell me!"

Meg hesitated before turning to her friend, a stony expression settling over her features. "I have no idea what you are talking about. I had a slight dizzy turn this morning, probably from not having had enough breakfast, and now I have a blister on my hand from the new gloves. Honestly, Allie, I'm perfectly fine and you need to stop carrying on like some old woman. Now, if it's all right with you, I am going back to my cottage to have a shower and change. Thanks for the game."

Allie blew out a breath. As she walked slowly back to her own cottage, she pondered how on earth she was going to get to the bottom of Meg's behaviour.

Chapter 2

Seated on a blanket under the shade of a large tree overlooking the verdant golf course, Bella Fiorisi and her partner Pat Campbell were taking advantage of the surprisingly warm late winter's morning. Bella watched as Pat unpacked their basket, taking out a thermos and a container of snacks.

"You know, I think the worst of the winter weather may be over," Bella said. "I'm getting so heartily sick of the cold. I can hardly wait for some warmth and sunshine again."

Pat tucked a rug gently around Bella and eased herself down next to her. Taking Bella in her arms, Pat settled them against the tree.

"You do know you say that every spring?" she teased.

"Well, it's true. There is something so magical about spring, seeing the buds appearing, feeling all that new life just waiting to explode. Even the air smells different." Closing her eyes, she took a deep breath, taking in the scent of the freshly mown grass and the sounds of the birds in the tree above them.

"So, are you feeling OK?" Pat asked.

Bella nodded. "It's so wonderful to no longer feel sick from the radiation treatment." Sitting up, she turned to Pat. Placing her hands on either side of Pat's face, Bella leant in.

"But not nearly as good as being told they believe the cancer has gone," she whispered.

Pat leant her forehead against Bella's. "So, explain to me again why you want to go ahead with the chemo? I just don't understand why you would put yourself through that treatment. It makes no sense."

Bella dropped her hands and felt her good mood quickly evaporating. She desperately wanted Pat to understand, and they had been arguing the pros and cons constantly since she'd made the decision several days ago. She felt if she had to explain it again she would go crazy.

"*Cara,* I need to do this. I've tried to explain, but sometimes I think you just don't want to hear me. The treatment will give me added protection, just in case there is something the doctors can't see. What is so damn hard to understand about that?" Bella asked, moving out of Pat's arms and wrapping the rug tightly around her shoulders.

She watched as Pat picked up a leaf and started shredding it.

"I want to help. I want to understand and support you, but…" Pat faltered.

Bella shook her head. "I'm tired, Pat. I really can't talk about this anymore. Let's not ruin this lovely morning. Please, *cara.*"

Hearing voices in the distance, both women looked across as Meg and Allie pulled their golf clubs towards the course. Bella watched them banter, Allie's laughter and the obvious playfulness of the moment helping to ease her mood.

They watched quietly as the women set up for their game. Meg's swing was strong and sure, and Bella followed the small white ball as it arced gracefully before falling on the fairway.

"Meg's a damn fine player," Pat said quietly. "I don't know why she never played professionally."

"You know, *cara*, sometimes people do things, like play golf, just for fun," Bella replied lightly.

Pat gave a small smile. "Are you possibly suggesting that I might have a compulsive competitive streak?"

"Mmmmm…maybe just a tiny bit," Bella agreed. "You know, you should start playing again. You played every week before I got sick and now you don't play at all. Meg and Allie would love you to join them, and you need a break from caring for me. I can manage by myself for a few hours."

Bella watched the emotions play across Pat's face and felt her heart sink. Since her treatment had begun, Pat had rarely left her side morning or night. Frustrated and increasingly irritated by all the fuss, Bella was at a loss for how to relieve the growing pressure. In an attempt to break the bleak mood that was threatening to ruin their morning, she once again moved close and leant her head on Pat's shoulder.

"Tell me our story?" she asked quietly.

Pat looked down at her with a smile. "How many times have we told this story to each other?" she asked, gently stroking Bella's face.

"I could hear it a million times and never grow tired of it. You tell it and suddenly we are young again. Please, *cara*, just once more."

Pat took her hand, and Bella saw the love in her eyes.

"Well, you'd better get comfortable," Pat advised. "It's a long story."

Bella sat up and repositioned herself against her lover's chest.

Wrapping her arms securely around Bella, Pat began the story she had told so many times before. "Forty-five years ago, we were both lucky enough to be working for the same company in Melbourne. You were the director's secretary and I had just been hired in the warehouse. One morning, not long after I started, I was asked to drop some paperwork upstairs. The person I had to deliver it to was away, and someone suggested I leave it with you." Pat paused, smiling as her memory replayed the familiar scene.

"I will never forget the first time I saw you sitting at your typewriter. You looked up and smiled at me and it was as if I forgot how to breathe. You were the most beautiful woman I had ever seen."

Bella chuckled at the memory. "*Cara*, I remember wondering if you were ill. You stood there, not saying a word, just staring at me. And then you just pushed this paperwork at me and fled before I could say a word to you."

Pat shrugged. "Well, I was so incredibly awkward and shy, I just wanted the ground to swallow me up."

"But you persevered," Bella reminded her.

Pat laughed. "Oh yes, but that's because I couldn't get the memory of you out of my head, and I realised I needed to be braver. I kept trying to find reasons to take paperwork upstairs. I would 'accidentally' bump into you at lunch time; if you smiled at me, my day was so much brighter, and when you went on holidays, I was miserable."

"Meanwhile," Bella interrupted, "I was trying to quietly find out who this handsome, shy woman was. Every time I tried to talk to you, though, you ran away."

"I was falling in love with you and had no idea how to deal with it," Pat murmured into Bella's hair

"And you never said a word to me," Bella whispered.

Pat shrugged again. "It never occurred to me that you might feel the same way. I was terrified you would find out and laugh at me."

Bella turned and prodded Pat gently. "Until the night of the storm, when you drove me home and I kissed you. Then you weren't so shy,"

"Oh, is that so?" Pat raised an eyebrow. "And just exactly who's telling this story?"

Bella laughed. "OK. I was just moving to the good bit."

"Well, it wasn't easy, was it?" Pat asked, settling them back against the tree. "Your strict Italian family almost had you on a curfew. I look back on that period and still wonder that they didn't discover we were lovers. I was so terrified they would find out and your brother would shoot me, or that someone at work would find out and we would both get sacked."

"And it wasn't just them," Bella reminded her. "Remember when we finally moved to Sydney? We thought we would be able to live freely, but even there it was a life of hidden nightclubs and dinners at close friends' houses. It was so hard to know who we could trust. Telling our straight friends and colleagues that we were flatmates; having to pretend to another life. It all felt so cheap and dirty. And in the background, so many friends who lost their jobs, their children, got arrested and beaten up. When you look at life now, it's hard to believe that we all lived in that constant fear."

"Remember our first Sydney Mardi Gras?" Pat asked.

Bella nodded, squeezing Pat's hand. "You were watching the parade and crying. When someone asked you why, you said it was because you were so happy."

"I couldn't believe it. Everything we fought for was right there, marching in all its flamboyance down Oxford Street. It was as if we had made it through all that pain and uncertainty and come out stronger and happier than we could ever have dreamt possible."

Bella turned. Taking Pat's hands, she chose her words carefully. "You know, that's how I feel about my cancer. I need to fight this, *cara*, with everything I have in me. It may not be enough, but if not, I need to know I gave it everything I could and have no regrets." Seeing the growing panic her words were causing, she softened her tone. "You and I have been through so much together. If I could spare you this pain I would, but the truth is, I can't do this without you."

"I just hate that it will continue to make you so sick," Pat said, anguished.

Bella once again leant back into Pat's arms. She felt the sun on her face and wished that time would just stop, allowing them to stay in this moment forever.

"We are nearly there, *cara*. We have to believe that this will be the turning point for us."

Bella felt the solid body of her lover as Pat took a deep breath. A moment passed before she heard the whispered words against her ear. "Well, if that's what you really want, I will be beside you every step of the way."

Chapter 3

Sparrow Hopkins sat in the small rotunda, gazing out into the surrounding gardens. Dappled sunlight filtered through the trees, creating patterns on the well-manicured lawns. Several gardeners were working on the nearby flower beds, and a slight breeze brought with it the rich aroma of freshly turned earth.

Sparrow looked down at the intricate embroidery in her lap. Her grandmother had first taught her this delicate art when she was a child and she'd never lost the love for it. She'd always found the practice soothing, allowing her mind to wander whilst stitching glorious works of art.

As she sewed, Sparrow thought back over the last twelve months. Being at OWL's Haven, had given her so much joy. The warm welcome she had been shown by the community had revived her personality and for the first time in years, she felt genuinely happy.

Callie, one of the resident cats, wandered in and rubbed her sleek tortoiseshell body against Sparrow's leg. Theoretically, she belonged to Louise and Caro, but her sociable nature had various residents trying to claim her as their own. As for Callie, she managed to share herself with everyone whilst graciously declining to belong to anyone, a feline trait that Sparrow greatly admired.

Bending down, she stroked the soft fur, smiling as Callie rolled over for a tummy rub.

"Hello there."

Sparrow looked up to see Daphne Williams standing at the entrance.

"Hello," she replied with delight. Noticing Daphne's hesitation, Sparrow beckoned her in.

"I'm not intruding, am I?" Daphne asked, taking a seat on the sofa next to her.

Sparrow shook her head. "No, not at all, Callie and I are just enjoying the day."

Callie rose and walked over to observe the willie wagtails swooping around the garden.

Daphne shook her head, watching the cat. "She hasn't got a chance of even getting near those little fellows. They'll drive her crazy and as soon as she gets close, they'll fly off laughing."

Callie's tail flicked as the birds swooped even closer to the bougainvillea growing around the sides of the rotunda.

"Sounds like my first girlfriend." Sparrow chuckled.

Intrigued, Daphne turned to face her, leaning back and stretching her long legs out in front of her. "Really? That sounds like a story. What happened?"

Recommencing her stitching, Sparrow smiled. "I was in my mid-twenties and had only recently accepted I was gay. I'd had a few liaisons, but was waiting to be romanced and wooed. We met at a party and at the end of the evening she made a huge song and dance about wanting to take me out. Wouldn't take no for an answer. Honestly, I thought I was going to have to leave town. She plied me with chocolates and flowers, took me out to dinner, tried to convince me that I was the only girl for her. I'd heard rumours about her 'love them and leave them' history, so I resisted for as long as I could, but I was young, and she was incredibly good looking and very funny. I did so want to believe everything she told me. She was in the Navy and was stationed nearby. All very hush-hush in those days, though. Couldn't let on that she was a lesbian. Finally one night, after a particularly romantic evening and rather too much wine, I said yes."

Sparrow looked at Daphne, who was watching her intently.

"Well it was quite amazing for about four weeks; I fell head over heels in love with her. But then the phone calls and dinner invitations slowed and the flowers stopped altogether. The next thing I knew she was chasing some other young woman, and I was left nursing a broken heart."

"Damn," said Daphne softly.

Sparrow nodded. "Damn indeed. I was so cross with myself. I should have known it wasn't a serious relationship for her, but…well, you do rather hope, don't you?"

Bored with the birds, Callie strolled back over and leapt nimbly onto the sofa between the two women.

Daphne gave the cat a gentle scratch. "So what happened next? Did you meet someone else?"

Embroidery forgotten, Sparrow looked into the distance as she remembered. "Well, you never think you are going to recover from your first love, do you? But several years later I fell in love with the most wonderful woman, and the two of us had such a life together. We travelled the world and saw things I'll never forget. Over twenty years together; then one day, out of the blue, she comes home and says she's leaving. No ifs, buts or maybes. Despite me begging her, she refused to tell me why, and I never found out the reason." Sparrow looked across and saw the shock on Daphne's face. "She had been quite ill several months before, and I often suspected that she might have discovered she had a terminal illness and couldn't bring herself to tell me. After she left, despite all our efforts, neither I nor any of her friends were able to find her. In the end, I just stopped looking."

Daphne released a breath. "How the hell did you cope?"

Sparrow smiled sadly. "I nearly went crazy wondering if it was something I had done; I didn't think I'd ever be the same again." Taking up her embroidery once more, Sparrow continued, "Still, one thing I have learnt is that no matter how much you might not want it to, life goes on. So, after three years of feeling sorry for myself, I picked myself up, dusted myself off and decided I had better get back into life. My friends, of course, wanted me go out and try to meet other women, but it was all a bit silly. I was too old to go through all that dating routine again, and I wasn't meeting anyone who I felt even remotely attracted to anyway, so after several failed attempts, I just stopped accepting invitations." Sparrow grimaced as she remembered the many awkward encounters. "I spent the next fifteen years alone. Not unhappy, but..." she paused, looking directly at Daphne, "not alive, not like I feel here. It was as if I was just...going through the motions. Now, when I look back, I don't recognise that me. She feels like someone else. Does that make sense?"

Daphne nodded thoughtfully. "Absolutely. I've always thought that there's something about OWL's that allows you to rediscover your spirit. I think it happens to all the women when they first arrive. It's the magic of being surrounded by a community of lesbians. It's okay to let down the guard rails of our emotions, because finally, we're safe. No-one is going to be offended by what we do or say, no-one is going to be titillated by our affection. We are surrounded by our people, women who love women. Why wouldn't our spirits soar?"

As they gazed at each other intently, Sparrow felt goosebumps brush her skin.

Callie stood, bumping her head against Daphne's hand.

Blinking, Daphne stood abruptly and looked at her watch. "Heavens, I should go. I have to call in on some friends...organise a fishing trip," she stammered.

Perplexed by the sudden change in Daphne's demeanour, Sparrow rose too.

Daphne gazed at her shyly. "Thank you for sharing your story with me. You're an incredibly brave woman."

Sparrow shook her head at the compliment. "I'm just glad I'm here now," she admitted as Daphne turned to leave.

Daphne stopped, looked back and gave Sparrow a sweet smile. "So am I."

Chapter 4

ALLIE WAS STANDING NEAR THE door of the library, studying the cover of the book she'd ordered, when she was grabbed from behind by two strong arms.

"Hey, sexy...you going my way?"

Allie laughed as Leslie Barlow linked an arm through hers.

"Well now, I'm not sure. It just might depend on where the two of us end up," she answered, bumping hips.

"I was wondering if you were going to the Tupperware presentation tonight?" Leslie asked, gesturing to the flyer on the library's notice board.

Leslie, resident joker at OWL's Haven, was in her mid-sixties, tall and lanky with short grey hair. Allie found her madcap personality to be a breath of fresh air.

"You are joking, aren't you? Tupperware?" Allie gave a snort of derision. "I don't think so."

"Oh come on, it'll be fun, I went to one in town a few weeks ago, with some of the other residents, and it was terrific. Helen talked to the consultant afterwards and asked her to do a presentation for us here." Leslie looked around and lowered her voice. "You should see some of the products they're bringing out now. Some of them could have very interesting alternative uses," she said, wiggling her eyebrows.

Allie slapped her on the arm, laughing. "Oh yes, you wish."

"I've talked Meg into coming," Leslie said, as if that settled the question, "as well as Daphne, Sparrow and a crowd of others."

"They do know what to expect, don't they?" asked Allie in surprise. "I mean, a Tupperware presentation isn't exactly a girls' night out."

"Yep, they know, and Meg said she's not coming without alcohol."

Allie chuckled, then blew out a sigh and gazed wistfully at the new book in her hand, seeing her carefully planned evening disappear under Leslie's persistence.

"Oh, all right, if they're all going to be there, I suppose you better count me in as well," she finally agreed.

"Excellent! It starts at six pm in the games room. Damn," she said, checking her watch, "I've got to go, but trust me, it's going to be fun so don't be late."

Leslie waved as she hurried off, and Allie watched her stride quickly out of the library. Knowing Leslie as she did, a fun night meant more than just a straightforward presentation, and she wondered what exactly her crazy friend had up her sleeve.

———— ⊰✦⊱ ————

Allie looked around with surprise at the number of people already gathered a good fifteen minutes before the scheduled time. A crowd of women clustered around a display table, inspecting an array of Tupperware products. Spying Meg talking to several residents at the refreshments table, Allie walked over to say hello.

"I have to ask," Meg greeted as she joined them, "since when have you been an aficionado of Tupperware? I thought you hated the stuff? I was stunned when Leslie told me this morning that you were coming to this."

Allie frowned in confusion. "What? She only mentioned it to me today after lunch. I have to say, I was just as surprised to hear you were coming."

"Well I only came because she told me you were going to be here," grumbled Meg.

"Speak of the devil," Allie said as Leslie made her way over to their group.

"Hi, glad you all made it..." Suddenly aware of the looks Meg and Allie were giving her, she stopped. "What?" she asked, flicking her gaze between the two of them.

"You told me this morning that you had already spoken to Allie about this evening and assured me she was coming," said Meg deliberately.

"Ahhh..." Leslie coloured slightly. "Yes, well...you know. I thought I had and then I realised I hadn't... But hey! You're both here now and we'll all have a great night. I'd love to chat, but I've got to go and help set up. I promise you, though, you won't regret coming."

She gave them a wink and rushed off before either woman could chastise her further.

Watching her walk away, Allie shook her head. "I swear that woman could sell the Sydney Harbour Bridge."

"Twice, to the same person," added Meg with a chuckle. After grabbing their glasses, they made their way through the crowd to claim seats close to the presentation area.

"Hello you two," said Daphne, sitting down next to Allie. "I must say I'm surprised to see you here. I didn't believe Leslie when she said you were both coming."

Meg raised an eyebrow. "It's a long story," she said. "How did she talk you into this fiasco?"

"I suspect she hypnotised me, because I have absolutely no idea what possessed me to say yes. However," she said, bringing out her flask, "if it all gets too boring, I have brought reinforcements."

"A woman after my own heart," chuckled Meg as she passed Allie a glass of wine.

A few minutes later, Helen Macintosh called out to the crowd, "Thank you, ladies, thank you! If you could all take your seats, we can get this presentation underway." Smiling, Helen turned to the woman standing next to her. "I'd like to introduce Jan Meredith, who will be our presenter tonight. Jan has worked for Tupperware for many years and gave a wonderful presentation that I attended a few weeks ago, in Berry. I am sure we're all thrilled that she's been kind enough to make a presentation here at OWL's Haven," she gushed, smiling at Jan flirtatiously.

Jan, an attractive woman in her late forties who obviously took pride in her appearance, smiled back. A green tailored skirt suit, soft green silk blouse and a gorgeous pair of patent leather dress pumps flattered her svelte figure.

"Thank you so much, Helen, for that lovely welcome, and good evening ladies! It is wonderful to see so many of you here tonight." Picking up one of the items on the table, she gestured towards the audience. "Tupperware is so well known in households around Australia that I would like to bet that each of you here tonight has used at least one of our products at some stage in your life. It may have been a mixing bowl, or one of our classic storage containers. While these are the standard products that everyone is familiar with, tonight I am going to introduce you to our new range of products: sleek, modernised and incredibly functional."

Daphne turned to Allie, rolling her eyes as she whispered, "It is Tupperware she's selling, isn't it?"

"I'm waiting for the free set of steak knives," Meg murmured drily.

Jan continued extolling the virtues of her products, and soon her promotion of the beauty and practicality of plastic kitchenware became tedious. Women began to shuffle in their chairs, while a series of coughs, like a rolling wave, ran through the room.

"If this continues," Meg said sotto voce, "I am going to need a great deal more wine."

"I wonder if I could have a member of the audience to assist me with the rest of this presentation?" Jan asked.

Before she had finished speaking, Leslie sprang from her seat, almost pushing Helen down in her rush to get to the stage.

Meg and Allie exchanged looks.

"Uh-oh, what's she up to?" Allie asked quietly.

"No idea," Meg replied, "but it'll probably be worth watching."

Glad to have the audience's attention once more and with a beaming Leslie at her side, Jan continued, "Now ladies, I know that there are many of you out there who enjoy cooking, and with this range of Tupperware products, you can enjoy the benefits of your creations even more. How many of you have experienced the disappointment of putting in all that culinary effort, only to open your storage container a couple of days later and discover that all you have left is a handful of stale tarts?"

Meg, who was in the process of taking a mouthful of wine, swallowed the wrong way and started coughing so badly that Allie had to thump her on the back. A collective chuckle rose from the other women in the room.

"Oh," said Leslie in a sultry tone, "nothing worse than a stale tart. I always insist that my tarts are fresh and moist."

Seemingly unaware of the reaction from the audience, Jan beamed at her assistant. "You are so right, and with the Tupperware range, we have several different sizes of containers. Just pop your tarts into one of these tightly sealed containers and you need never eat another soft, dry tart again."

Unable to speak herself, Allie was aware of Daphne shaking with laughter next to her as she stammered, "Soft, dry tarts. Did she really say that?"

Meg shook her head, the laughter still bubbling out of her. "By the look of her, I suspect Leslie is enjoying this way too much."

While mostly maintaining a perfectly serious expression, Leslie continued to assist Jan, her subtly nuanced comments keeping the audience thoroughly entertained.

Her enthusiasm growing at the audience's apparent enjoyment of the presentation, Jan picked up a small plastic device with four small clips attached.

"Now, Leslie, I bet you can't imagine what this is for?" she asked.

Leslie examined it carefully, keeping her expression blank.

"Well, I'm not sure," she offered as she showed it to the audience, "but these little clips on the end are certainly intriguing."

As Jan took the gadget back, Allie's imagination was busy inventing all sorts of unorthodoxed uses for the implement.

Jan leant in to her audience conspiratorially. "Now, I don't know about you ladies, but I have always hated putting my hands inside poultry cavities. Too many times, those spaces are just way too small for even our delicate hands to fit. This clever little tool," she said, straightening up and displaying it, "expands the entrance of any cavity to maximum stretch. You simply place the clips around the edge of the bird's cavity, stretch the opening and these plastic sides lock in to hold the cavity open. Then, you take this tubing," she added, holding it up to the now engrossed audience, "and fill it with your stuffing, tamping it down as you go. In no time at all, you have a cavity filled to capacity, all the while keeping your hands clean and dry."

The women sat spellbound, every one watching with rapt attention.

Jan continued blithely, "Of course, on occasion, you may need to oil the cavity to ensure that the inside is nice and moist." Turning to her display case, she pulled out a large rubber roast chicken and a small bottle of oil.

"Oh good grief, she even comes with her own props," Meg whispered to Allie.

"So here we have our small, dry cavity," Jan said, indicating the back end of the chicken. "All we need to do is pop these clips around the opening of the cavity and stretch it as far as possible. The clips, of course, are made of plastic, so as not to tear the flesh."

Several women in the audience squirmed in their chairs as she placed the device on the chicken. When the sides were locked into place, she displayed that the cavity was at full stretch.

Allie watched in fascination, her wine forgotten.

"Then when it is stretched as far as possible, I will oil the outside of the tubing," Jan went on, proceeding to brush the tubing until it glistened. She beamed as she showed them her handiwork. "Once that is done, I slip the tubing in like this and rub it gently around the cavity to ensure it is also lightly lubricated. Now I can proceed to fill it with stuffing." Jan demonstrated with dry pasta, tamping it into the interior of the chicken.

Meg put her hand on Allie's arm and leant in to whisper, "If she keeps going on like this, I swear some of these old girls are going to have a coronary. This is probably the most action some of them have seen in fifteen years!"

Smothering a laugh, Allie quickly glanced around the room. "I must say, there do appear to be some that are paying very close attention."

"When all the stuffing is in place," Jan was saying, "you undo the clips, give a gentle tug and the cavity expander slips right out, leaving your chicken stuffed and your hands clean."

Leslie cleared her throat, motioning towards the now distended chicken. "That must be a very popular item in your range," she said, trying to keep a straight face.

"I have to say," Jan replied, "we have been surprised at the number of women who have ordered this. It has been on our top ten list since it was introduced several months ago. Although the stretching device is small, it is surprisingly strong and comes in three different sizes, from small to large."

"I am sure that many women could find...*all* sorts of uses for it," Leslie agreed, looking out to the audience.

"Well, we at Tupperware pride ourselves on our versatility and would love to hear from women who find other uses for our products."

Allie blinked rapidly and sat back in her chair. "Good Lord, I swear I'll never be able to look at a chicken the same way again."

By now the noise level had escalated, as the ribald comments amongst the audience increased.

Looking around the room, Allie turned to Meg. "I don't think the lovely Jan has any idea of the reactions she's causing."

Meg grinned, nodding towards the stage. "No, but Leslie does. This is obviously why she wanted us all to come tonight."

Delighted by the women's enthusiasm, Jan selected another product from the display table. "Now, ladies, here's something that the bakers amongst you won't want to miss. It's a new product in our range and it allows you to pipe cream or icing in a pretty and decorative manner. Also, the unique style means that it's drip free."

Handing the device to her assistant, Jan asked her to display it closer to the audience.

"Oh, what a useful gadget, Jan," Leslie gushed, showing it to several women in the front row. "So, effectively, I could fill this with honey, or melted chocolate, and pipe it exactly where I needed it?" Turning to the audience, she waggled her eyebrows. "And there would be no danger of it spilling on the sheets...er...I mean, bench top?"

"Yes exactly," beamed Jan. "And it also comes with its own attachments for those of you who wish to do more detailed artwork."

"Oh," exclaimed Leslie, holding up the attachments, "look at these little plugs! I'm sure they could be put to use in all sorts of ways."

The growing ripples of laughter caused Jan to hesitate; a look of uncertainty crossed her face. She turned to collect another appliance from the table, and when she faced them again, her smile was fixed firmly in place once more.

"Now, for those of you who have problems with your wrists getting sore from too much beating, we have the 'Quick Flick'. This is guaranteed to give you creamy results in half the time of a normal beater."

"Oh, ladies," Leslie said, grabbing the item and holding it close to her chest, "the answer to all our dreams! Imagine how incredibly useful this will be." Turning to Jan, she shook her head and sighed. "My wrists often get sore from too much beating." Then with a quick smile, she asked sweetly, "Is it battery operated?"

"No," Jan hesitated, gazing with bewilderment at her increasingly rowdy audience. "Its secret is all in the new angled design."

"Oh, yes," Leslie continued, clasping Jan's arm, "I am sure we women are all aware that we have to have just the right angle for creamy results. Well, this little treasure's certainly going on my shopping list."

The other women in the room had by now given up all pretence of decorum. As the laughter increased, Jan narrowed her eyes at Leslie.

"Uh-oh," Daphne muttered to Allie, "I think Jan's just woken up to Leslie's game!"

Forcibly removing Leslie's hand from her arm, Jan straightened her jacket.

"Why don't we look at our range of kitchen implements," she began, edging Leslie away from the table while picking up one of the spatulas from the display. Raising her voice over the hubbub, she forged on, "Tupperware has just released our new lighter spatula. It's designed to be more flexible, but has the strength to be even more effective."

Dodging around Jan, Leslie quickly grabbed one and smacked it lightly against her hand several times.

"Mmm," she said throatily. "You know, Jan, you're absolutely right. Tupperware has become so much more functional."

Just when Allie felt that Jan was about to totally lose her professional demeanour, Helen rose and marched up to the stage. Placing her hand protectively on Jan's arm, she glared quickly at Leslie before turning to the audience.

"I think we would all like to thank Jan for the wonderful presentation she gave tonight. It was incredibly kind of her to take time out of her busy schedule to show us these excellent products. I am sure we would like to give her a round of applause," she announced with authority.

The women clapped heartily and Leslie, who was now standing behind both Jan and Helen, gave several bows. At the renewed cheering, Jan beamed.

"Thank you all very much. I am so glad you enjoyed the evening. There are order forms on the table for those who wish to purchase any of tonight's products, as well as copies of our catalogues," she announced. "I will also leave my business card for those who wish to call me later for a personal demonstration."

"Oh, good grief, she is going from bad to worse," gasped Daphne when the audience erupted again. "My stomach hurts from laughing so much."

The three women sat back in their chairs, watching Helen help Jan pack up the merchandise. When Leslie leant in to help, Helen slapped her hand away and glared at her angrily.

With an exaggerated shrug of puzzlement, Leslie casually sauntered over to her friends. Throwing herself into a vacant chair in front of them, she grinned.

"Now, didn't I tell you that tonight would be fun?" she asked.

Allie wiped her eyes. "You are positively evil, but I have to admit, that was one of the funniest evenings I've spent in a long time."

"Well, I ended up at the Women's Institute presentation she gave in Berry. Yeah, I know, don't ask," she added in response to Meg's quizzical look. "Anyway, afterwards I thought it might be fun to have one here and asked Helen if she thought Jan would do it. She positively quivered with excitement at the thought of the two of them spending more time together. Because I'd been to the earlier one, I knew Jan would ask for an assistant, and all I had to do was beat Helen to the stage. Once I got up there it was a piece of cake," she smirked.

"Doesn't she know we're a bunch of lesbians?" Daphne asked in amazement.

Leslie shook her head and accepted the glass of wine Meg handed her. "No, I don't think she has any idea, which is what made it all so funny. She knew something was going on, but I still don't think she's figured it out. I can't believe Helen didn't say something to her."

Women began coming up to congratulate Leslie on her performance. The general consensus was that it had been a night to remember. Before long, Helen came barrelling towards them like a galleon under full sail, her face red with outrage. The howls of laughter that greeted her approach only escalated her fury.

"Uh-oh, here's trouble. Now you're in for a good tongue lashing," warned Daphne as she collapsed back into her chair.

"That was unforgivable behaviour tonight," Helen gasped, almost spitting the words out as she waved her finger under Leslie's nose. "Poor Jan gave up her time to come here to give us this presentation and all you could do was make fun of her. Do you know she is one of the top five presenters in the state for Tupperware? We were so lucky to have her here. Honestly, it was the sort of childish behaviour I would have expected from you." Swinging around to confront the other three women, Helen continued, "I expect you three are co-conspirators?"

"Oh put a sock in it, Helen," Meg snapped. "If she was half the saleswoman you say she is, she would have done her research and known that tonight was going to be a lesbian audience. Unless you are totally stupid, you don't start talking about tarts, beaters and cavity expanders in a room full of lesbians and not expect a reaction. Besides, Leslie made it entertaining, Jan will get plenty of sales for the beater thingy and you got her business card so you can call her later for a 'personal demonstration'. All in all," Meg said, raising her glass, "I'd say it was an exceptionally successful evening."

Outraged, Helen spun on her heel and marched off.

Taking a swallow of wine, Leslie chuckled. "Poor Jan. I wonder if she'll ever discover what went wrong."

"I wouldn't think so," said Meg. "She'll probably put it all down to senility or dementia."

"Hers or ours?" asked Daphne, laughing.

An hour later, Allie stretched and stood, swaying a little on her feet. "Well, I haven't had that much fun in ages, but I think it's about time for me to go to bed."

"I think someone may have had a little too much to drink," surmised Meg, grabbing her arm.

"Nonsense. I'm perfectly fine," Allie replied thickly. "Besides, how can we get drunk on half a bottle of wine?"

Daphne laughed. "Allie, I count two empty bottles under Meg's chair—and don't look at me, because I've only been drinking whiskey."

"Good grief, Meg, did you get me drunk?" Allie asked crossly.

Meg stood and put an arm around her. "Hush now. I'll walk you home, you poor old lush."

"That's good, because I might need a little bit of help."

After saying their goodnights, Meg walked Allie to her door and let them both into the cottage.

"Are you OK to get ready for bed?" Meg asked.

Leaning against the bathroom door, Allie nodded. "Can you stay a while?" she asked.

"Of course I can, darling. Go and get changed."

Several minutes later, Allie emerged from the bathroom smelling of soap and toothpaste. As she settled in bed, Meg handed her a large glass of water.

"Oh wonderful, just what I need," Allie said.

Meg sat on the bed, watching her closely. "How do you feel, sweetie?"

Allie giggled. "Fine, except I can't stop thinking about that poor, damned chicken."

They both dissolved into laughter.

"And don't forget that beater thingy," Meg hooted.

"For extra creamy results," Allie spluttered, hiccuping.

Placing the now empty glass on the bedside table, Meg shook her head. "I think people are going to be talking about tonight for quite a while. Best entertainment I've had in months."

Allie took Meg's hand. "We do have some laughs, you and I, don't we?"

Linking her fingers through Allie's, Meg nodded. "The best times of my life have been with you," she said quietly.

Allie yawned and snuggled down into the duvet. "I do love you, Meg," she said sleepily.

Meg bent down to kiss her cheek. "I love you too, darling," she replied softly. "Sleep well. I'll see you in the morning."

* * *

The next morning, Allie groaned when she heard Meg let herself into the cottage.

"How are you feeling?" Meg called down the hall.

"How am I feeling?" she responded as her friend entered the bedroom. "Well, if the jackhammer in my head and the merry-go-round in my stomach would both stop, I might feel vaguely human. Exactly how much wine did I drink last night?"

"Oh for heaven's sake, it was just a few bottles. You've had triple that amount in the past and not even blinked. Why, just last week we polished off two bottles of red with dinner."

"Yes but that night, if you remember, you drank most of it; I only had a couple of glasses." Allie squinted up at Meg through one eye. "How the hell are you so damned chipper anyway? You drank a lot more than I did."

"Practice makes perfect. Now, are you going to get out of bed so we can get ready? We don't have a lot of time, and I don't want to miss anything."

She lay there looking at Meg, trying to remember what could possibly be important enough to make her want to stand upright.

"Um, remind me again..."

"Honestly, Allie," said Meg in exasperation. "Today is Wednesday and the first day of Zumba classes for the season. I'm told that the teacher is gorgeous and looks like a goddess in a leotard. So, go and jump into the shower whilst I find your exercise clothes."

Allie lay there bewildered, then started to laugh. "Darling Meg, this trainer, goddess though she may be, is probably forty years younger than we are. Have you considered what on earth we would even do in the unlikely event that she suddenly discovers that she has an attraction for older women? Good grief, I'm likely to have a coronary just thinking about it."

"That's the trouble with you, Allie Richards," Meg snapped, slamming the wardrobe door. "Just because you're in your sixties, you think you're written off. Well, you might think like that but don't expect me to. I'm going to the gym and if she smiles at me, I'm damn well smiling back. If you can drag your ancient bones out of bed, I'll see you there. If not, I'll see you later." Meg turned and stomped angrily out of the cottage.

Despite her spinning head, Allie sat up, stunned. What on earth had prompted Meg to turn on her like that? Allie thought back to the episode on the golf course. In all their years of friendship, they had rarely quarrelled; now Allie was really concerned. She knew she would have to tread carefully in her efforts to discover what exactly was upsetting her old friend. In the meantime, she supposed, sighing, a pretty face would cheer her up and some exercise might be just the thing for her hangover.

Chapter 5

SPRING

CARO DROPPED HEAVILY ONTO THE leather sofa next to the desk where Louise was working on accounts.

"I've just dropped Bella and Pat back at their cottage and helped settle Bella into bed," she said despondently.

"How did she go today?" Louise asked.

"Well, she looks as if a puff of wind could blow her over, and I'm not sure how much more of this either of them can take. I think Pat's about ready to break."

Despite all that the nursing staff at the hospital tried to do for her, this last course of chemotherapy was making Bella incredibly ill. Louise, as owner and manager of OWL's Haven, was in regular contact with Bella's doctors to ensure that whatever she needed was available for her at home.

Louise put her pen down and studied her partner. Caro's distress was evident, and Louise rose to join her on the sofa. Caro sighed, resting her head on Louise's shoulder and taking her hand.

"I spoke to the nursing staff while Pat was getting Bella into the car. They think it would be a good idea for her to be admitted as a patient until she finishes the course. They're quite worried that she's having such a bad reaction this time round."

"There's no way Pat will let Bella go into hospital by herself, and I don't see the hospital letting Pat stay each time she has a treatment," Louise said softly. "How did Pat react to the suggestion?"

Caro grimaced. "They haven't mentioned it to either of them yet. I guess they didn't want to add more stress to an already really shitty day."

Louise sat thinking, an idea germinating in her mind. "There may be a way…"

"What are you thinking?" Caro asked, sitting up.

Louise stood. "Let's think outside the square." She started pacing, her default action when she was trying to think. "The hospital wants Bella there so that they can monitor her more closely and look after her, right?"

She turned to Caro for confirmation.

"Yeah, pretty much."

Louise resumed her pacing, "…and we don't want Bella and Pat to be apart any more than they do, right?"

"Right."

Louise smiled and sat down on the arm of the sofa, running her fingers through Caro's hair. "So the solution is simple. We hire a trained nurse to look after Bella here. That way, she gets twenty-four-hour care, they don't have to be apart, Bella will be in her own home and both of them will have support from the residents and staff here."

Caro smiled and closed her eyes, relaxing as Louise's fingers gently massaged her head. "You are a genius. You know that don't you?" Opening her eyes, she hesitated as a thought hit her. "I hate to bring it up, but it might be pretty expensive. I don't know that Bella and Pat can afford it; you know how proud they both are."

Louise squeezed Caro's shoulder and stood to walk back to her desk. "I'll speak to the board and our insurers. There may be a way of offering a long-term payment plan at a slightly reduced rate. These women are family, and if we present the option properly, I think they will be happy to accept the extra help."

Caro stood and stretched, trying to roll the tension out of her shoulders. "Well, I think it's a brilliant idea. Let's hope they agree."

"I'll go and talk to them both later this afternoon," Louise replied, looking for her planner and trying to ignore the paperwork strewn across her desk.

Caro frowned. "You look tired, honey. Why don't you give yourself an early mark and come home so I can look after you? Take some breathing space before you go and see Pat and Bella. We could even see if Naomi can give us both a massage. Heaven knows I could use one; my back feels like a plank of wood."

Louise let out a long breath. There wasn't anything on her desk that couldn't wait until tomorrow and the thought of a massage and a few quiet hours with Caro sounded wonderful.

"That might just be the best offer I've had all day. You, me and a heavenly massage."

"With warmed scented oil, in a dimly lit room," added Caro in a sultry voice.

Louise rose and walked into her partner's arms. "I suggest you stop talking and we start moving now, or I'll turn around and lock this door and neither of us will be going anywhere for quite some time."

Chapter 6

ALLIE PLACED HER UNFINISHED BOOK on the side table and stretched out on the sofa. A low thrumming headache had made her tired and restless most of the afternoon. She put it down to the unseasonable heat of the last week. Allie hated sleeping without her window open, but even after dark, the heat had been relentless and her broken sleep was beginning to take a toll. She was resigned to closing her window and leaving the air conditioning on tonight in the hope that she would sleep through.

She was about to settle back to her book when she heard Meg letting herself into the cottage. They had traded door keys when they'd first moved in, and Allie often came home to find Meg waiting for her.

"Are you decent?" Meg called out, making her way down the hallway.

Allie laughed. "Would it make any difference?"

Meg entered the room and dropped onto the sofa. "No, probably not, but my mother brought me up to always ask." She fixed Allie with a mischievous grin. "So, what are you doing?"

Allie narrowed her eyes. She could see that Meg was up to something and wasn't at all that sure she wanted to find out what it was.

"Why?" she asked cautiously.

"Well," Meg leant forward to look Allie straight in the eye. "Myself, Daphne and a few of the other women have decided that it's such a gorgeous evening, we're going swimming—and I think you should come with us,"

Allie blinked. "Isn't the pool closed?" She glanced at her watch. "I mean, it's six-fifteen at night."

Meg waved her hand dismissively. "Oh, you are such an old stick in the mud. There are ways to get around things like that. Besides, you were complaining of a headache all afternoon. A swim will make you feel like a new woman, and as I keep telling you, if you're lucky you might find one," she added, laughing at her own joke.

"Meg…"

"Oh Allie, come on," Meg interrupted. "It'll be fun, and it's so damn hot! Just think, a nice cool swim… Please, for me?"

Allie shook her head and laughed. She had never been able to say no to Meg's madcap ideas and she had to admit that a swim did sound tempting. She placed her book on the table and rose from the sofa.

"All right, just let me get my costume."

Meg grabbed her arm. "No, no costumes. We're going skinny dipping."

"We're *what*?" Allie looked at her friend incredulously.

Meg stood, dismissing Allie's objections. "Just stop making a fuss and come on. We're meeting Daphne and the others at her place. Leslie's got some vodka too, in case we get thirsty. The others are bringing soft drinks and cheese and fruit. Have you got any of those delicious quiches left over?"

Allie groaned loudly as she followed Meg to the kitchen. "Oh Meg, this is such a bad, bad idea."

"Nonsense. We'll have a ball and it'll be fine. What could possibly go wrong with a quick swim and a few drinks?" Meg asked as she took the quiches out of the fridge.

"Oh, I don't know," muttered Allie, putting the small pastries in a container while Meg selected a bottle of wine. "But I'm sure we are about to find out."

They met up with the other skinny dippers outside Daphne's cottage, and the five of them quietly made their way to the pool. A fading twilight bathed the grounds with shadows, and the women watched in delight as an owl flew silently overhead. Lights were glowing over in the clubhouse, and they could hear faint strains of music.

Sparrow flicked on a small torch she had brought with her, checking that the darkened path ahead was clear.

"Keep the light low, Sparrow," Leslie said. "We don't want anyone to spot us."

Sparrow dipped the light as the women quickly crossed the lawn to the locked pool.

"Oh, I can almost feel that cool water against my skin already," Daphne whispered excitedly.

"I hate to be the voice of gloom, but how are we supposed to get in?" Allie asked. "In case you haven't noticed, there's a bloody big padlock on the gate and I'll tell you now, there is no way I am climbing that fence."

"More than one way to skin a cat," Daphne quipped, stepping forward. "Now, Sparrow, if you can just hold that torch just about there..."

Turning the padlock, she inserted a small, thin wire into the key barrel. The others watched, fascinated, as she very gently manipulated the wire inside the lock.

"Almost there," Daphne breathed. "Come on, baby... Yes." The padlock clicked open.

"Bloody brilliant," declared Meg. "Well done."

Daphne smiled triumphantly. "Like riding a bike, you never forget how to do the important things in life."

The women trooped into the pool enclosure, Daphne quietly closing the gate behind them. The all-weather pool was wonderfully private and small. Underwater lights glowed softly, making the still water appear incredibly inviting.

"All right ladies," said Meg, "let's get organised. For heaven's sake, remember not to turn any lights on."

Sparrow positioned the torch so there was just enough light to see what they were doing as they unpacked the food and drinks together with plates and utensils.

"This feels like those midnight feasts we used to have at boarding school," Sparrow whispered excitedly, looking at the tempting array of food. "It's always so much more fun when it's illegal."

"So, what do we want to do first?" asked Meg. "Swim or eat and drink?"

"Probably more sensible to swim first and drink later, don't you think, Meg?" Allie answered. "Unless, of course, you plan on giving mouth to mouth resuscitation for the evening's finale."

Meg stuck her tongue out in response. "Ever the practical one." Pausing, she considered her friend carefully. "Though, I must say, now you mention it, I do like the thought of that mouth to mouth thing."

"Always good to keep up to date with the latest techniques, Meg," Daphne added with a snigger. "I'm a great believer that practice makes perfect."

"Well, ladies," Meg announced, peeling off her clothes, "you know what they say, last one in's a rotten egg."

With that, she winked at Allie and dived naked into the pool. Moments later, she was joined by a flurry of pale, naked bodies as the other women also abandoned their clothing and entered the water.

"Oh," swooned Daphne. "This is absolutely heavenly."

"I must say, there is something about not wearing a costume," Sparrow murmured, trying not to feel too self-conscious.

"Yep, really cools off your lady bits," added Leslie.

Daphne, who was in the process of quietly swimming her way over to Sparrow, swallowed a mouthful of water and came up spluttering. Sparrow took her arm, concerned.

"Are you all right?" she asked.

"Yes, I'm fine," gasped Daphne, forcing a smile. "Just swallowed some water the wrong way."

Across the pool, Allie nudged Meg and Leslie. "Is it my imagination, or do you think we might have ourselves a romance blossoming over there?"

The three of them looked over. Daphne and Sparrow were standing absolutely still, their bodies almost touching, completely focussed on each other.

"Well, it's very possible. Sparrow seemed hesitant to join us tonight until I mentioned Daphne would be coming as well," Meg replied.

Leslie smiled. "Well, I don't see any sign of hesitation now from either of them."

———✦✧✦———

Leslie swam over and grabbed a large beach ball from the side of the pool.

"Toss it to me," Daphne called quietly.

Daphne caught the ball and tossed it back, but before Leslie could reach it, Sparrow stretched out and intercepted. Allie almost had her hand on the ball when Meg lunged over and pushed her head under the water.

"That's cheating," Allie spluttered, laughing, as she resurfaced.

"You snooze, you lose," called Meg, tossing the ball back to Sparrow before grabbing Allie. "Let's make this interesting," she said to Leslie. "What say we break into two teams."

"But there's only five of us," Sparrow said.

"I'm happy to be referee," Leslie said. "I suggest Daphne and Sparrow versus Meg and Allie."

Sparrow turned to the others, who quickly agreed to the challenge.

"Let's make some rules," said Leslie. "If the ball touches the water or leaves the pool, it's a point against that side. First side to ten points loses. The main rule is, you are not allowed to drown each other. Let the games begin!"

The ball flew from side to side. The women lunged, leapt and laughed. The score was nine apiece, and Meg was getting ready to serve the ball. Watching her take aim, the much taller Daphne stood behind Sparrow and whispered into her ear. As the ball started to sail high over their heads, she put her hands around Sparrow's waist and lifted her clear out of the pool. Sparrow gave the ball a solid whack and watched with delight as it hit the water just out of reach of Allie's hand.

Daphne lowered Sparrow back into the water and gave her a kiss on the cheek. "Well done! That was a champion shot."

"It was your idea," Sparrow replied. "Did you see the expression on Meg's face as you lifted me out of the water? I thought she was going to drown, she was laughing so hard."

Allie swam over to them. "I'm sure that was cheating, but it was so damn funny I don't care."

"I don't know about the rest of you," declared Meg, "but I'm starving and all that splashing around has given me a thirst."

Slowly the women got out of the pool and padded over to the tables. Finding clothes and towels, they dried themselves off, dressed, and started preparing the food and drink.

"Well I think that takes care of this month's exercise. I had no idea I had that much energy," Sparrow chuckled. "This was a great idea, Meg."

"Well we wouldn't have been able to do it without Daphne's lock picking skills, so here's to her," Meg toasted, raising her glass.

Leslie smiled. "Should we ask exactly where you learnt to do that?"

Daphne winked at her. "The great school of life."

"Sounds a whole lot more interesting than the one I went to," Sparrow said quietly, arranging a plate of fruit and cheese.

"Did I hear you say earlier that you went to boarding school, Sparrow?" Meg asked, looking over the selection of food as she ran her fingers through her wet hair.

Sparrow nodded as she took a seat next to Daphne and poured them each a small glass of wine. "Yes, five years at a Catholic, all-girls boarding school in the middle of the English countryside, while my father was stationed at the Army base in Aldershot."

"Wow, so is it true about Catholic boarding schools? Are they hot beds of lesbian passion?" Leslie asked dramatically.

"Well, sort of. I mean, I did have a sort of a thing with another girl… Well, we just kissed a lot," Sparrow admitted, blushing.

Daphne passed her a biscuit with cheese. "What were the nuns like? Did they roam the corridors at night seeking out students engaging in illicit acts?"

Sparrow shook her head and laughed. "Well it wasn't so much that. It was more that they couldn't seem to cope with the day to day matters of life, as far as we girls were concerned."

Meg settled herself next to Allie. "Such as?" she queried with a frown.

"Well, for example. There was this lovely American girl in my class whose father was stationed at the same place as my dad. She arrived in the middle of the term and we became quite good friends. Being a Catholic school, the words 'period' and 'menstruation' were never used, so when we had our periods, we had to go to the nun in charge of the small shop and say, 'Sister, I have a headache.' She would then open a drawer and hand us a small parcel of modess pads, discreetly wrapped in brown paper."

Everyone laughed.

"Are you serious?" Allie asked in amazement.

"Yep, I swear. Unfortunately, though, no-one told Mandy, the American girl. One day she went to the shop and said, 'Sister, I have a headache,' and was duly given the parcel. Somewhat puzzled, she took it back to her room and unwrapped it. Apparently, she sat there for a while, rather perplexed, until she thought she figured out what she was supposed to do. Next thing we knew, she was walking into the classroom with the pad, which she had soaked in cold water, tied around her forehead."

The women erupted in gales of laughter.

"Honestly," Sparrow continued, still laughing at the memory, "I thought the nun teaching the class was going to have a coronary. I can still hear her. *'Amanda Douglas, get that THING off your head immediately and report to the headmistress.'* Mandy was completely bewildered by the whole episode. All she wanted was something for her headache. Meanwhile, once we recovered from the shock, the whole class was hysterical. I laughed so much I was nearly sick."

"So what did you ask for if you really did have a headache?" asked Daphne.

Sparrow chuckled. "Believe it or not, an aspirin. Poor kid, it wasn't her fault. When she was given the parcel, she just assumed that this was some weird British rite. She didn't want to ask, so she just used her head."

"Literally, it would seem," Meg said, smiling.

Leslie shook her head. "I'm still coming to terms with the picture of nuns wrapping modess pads in brown paper parcels."

"Good Lord, how did we survive our educations?" Daphne groaned.

"We were taught about reproduction with films of frogs mating," Allie offered, spearing a piece of sweet honeydew.

Puzzled, Daphne stared at her. "What? How on earth was that relevant?"

"I have no idea, but from that day onwards one of the girls refused to go swimming with boys, because she thought that was how you got pregnant. I often wonder how long it took her to figure it out," Allie replied, popping the piece of melon in her mouth.

"Kids today are so lucky. There is so much information out there now. I remember when I first realised I was gay, I thought I was the only one in the whole world. I didn't even know the name for what I felt. When I did find out, it was even worse. Good Catholic family—I was convinced I was going to burn in hell. I ended up leaving home rather than tell my parents. They probably would have kicked me out anyway," Sparrow said quietly.

"I knew from a very early age and did get kicked out of home." Seeing the shocked faces around her, Meg shrugged. "I never got on with my parents anyway. They were more interested in societal appearances than reality. However, I had a…" Meg paused with a small smile. "I think we called them 'maiden aunts' in those days. She was very rich, very rebellious and very loving, and spent four years nurturing my strength, identity and sense of adventure."

Allie squeezed Meg's hand. "Well, she sure did a damned fine job."

"When did you realise you were a lesbian, Allie?" Daphne asked, watching the interaction between her and Meg.

"Oh good Lord, believe it or not it was at a party in Kings Cross just after my twenty-third birthday. From the age of sixteen, all I heard from my parents was 'when you get married',' and all the girls I used to hang around with continually talked about boys and sex. Even after I finally got a boyfriend, I was still no clearer as to what all the fuss was about." Allie looked at Meg fondly. "Meg was the first lesbian I ever met, and once she introduced me to her friends, I started to realise that maybe men weren't the only option. There was a great club in Kings Cross that we went to quite regularly. They had an exotic dancer…"

"Delores, would you believe?" said Meg, rolling her eyes. The other women guffawed.

"Anyway," Allie continued, ignoring them, "she used to come and sit with us between breaks. She and I used to chat and she would give me dance lessons."

"Just in case she needed another career if the chef thing fell through," chuckled Meg, trying to keep a straight face.

Allie continued through the laughter, "So, one night we arrived and there was this amazing party happening at the club. Delores and I began dancing and...well, one thing led to another and I found myself upstairs in her apartment." Allie smirked. "I'll leave the rest up to your imagination."

Sparrow nudged her shoulder. "Sounds like a lot of fun."

"You got free dancing lessons, and Delores got the toaster oven. I think that's a very equitable lesbian exchange," Leslie concluded happily.

"And now here we all are in the first retirement village run specifically for lesbians. We've come a long way, baby," Allie said, clinking her glass with Meg's.

"Hear, hear," chorused the women, raising their glasses.

The women sat quietly talking amongst themselves, until finally Sparrow yawned. "I don't know about the rest of you, but I'm bushed."

Agreeing, the others rose and started packing up, collecting bottles and wrapping the leftover fruit and cheese. They checked to make sure they had left nothing behind before closing and locking the gate to the pool. As they walked slowly back to their homes, they talked quietly amongst themselves.

Meg linked her arm through Allie's and smiled at her. "So, are you glad you came tonight?"

Allie squeezed Meg's arm. "Yes, despite my fears, it was a wonderful night."

"You should let go more often. You know that don't you?"

Allie sighed. "I know, but I guess it's still hard. I'm just not wired like you. You're a 'feel the fear and do it anyway' kind of person; it's one of the things I've always loved about you. Sometimes I hate that I'm boring and always looking at the practical side of everything, but I suspect that it's too late for me to change now."

"Well, it does have its advantages, you know. Can you imagine if we were both like me? We'd have probably died thirty years ago."

Allie laughed. "Yes, I must say I've never regretted stopping you from flying under the Sydney Harbour Bridge back in your pilot days."

"Or that time you talked me out of entering the Dakar Rally," added Meg.

"I never understood why you wanted to do that. There we were, in our forties, and you wanted to go charging across the bloody desert in a car. Even...what was her name... Francoise, thought you were crazy."

"Ah yes, the beautiful Francoise," said Meg dreamily. "God, she was gorgeous."

"Yes, and she cost you a great deal of money, I seem to remember," Allie replied drily.

"And, like all beautiful things, she was truly worth every cent." Meg stopped and turned to take Allie's hands. "We should go back to Paris for a visit—just the two of us. Hot air ballooning over the French vineyards has been on my bucket list for years. I can't believe we haven't done that yet."

"Well I am sure that can be arranged, but can we talk about it tomorrow? I'm nearly asleep on my feet, and I can't possibly think about trips to Paris tonight."

Meg laughed and drew her into a hug as they paused in front of Allie's door. "Of course, darling. Sleep well and I'll see you in the morning."

Waving goodnight to the group, Allie let herself into her cottage. As she crawled into bed, she started to laugh. "Hot air balloons indeed."

Chapter 7

SPARROW SAT ON HER SOFA, surrounded by embroidery threads. A unique cushion design had caught her eye and she was trying to decide which of the myriad of colours laid out before her would be the best choice for the next stage of the design. She ran her hands over the threads, revelling in the rich hues of gold, red and green and the way they shone in the sunlight streaming through her window.

A knock at the door interrupted her concentration. She glanced at her watch and was taken aback to see that it was nearly three-thirty.

When she opened the door, she was delighted to see Daphne standing there.

"Hi, Sparrow. I'm not sure if you are busy, but I was going for a walk and I wondered if you would like to join me?"

"Oh, how wonderful. Yes, I'd love to." The sight of the object of her nascent fantasies standing in her doorway caused Sparrow's heart to race, leaving her uncharacteristically flustered. Realising she was just standing there, she motioned Daphne inside. "Sorry, please come in and I'll just get myself organised."

Daphne followed her into the living room.

"Sorry, I didn't mean to interrupt," she said, looking at the splash of colour the range of embroidery threads created on the sofa, "but it's such a lovely afternoon, and well..."

As Sparrow turned and smiled up at her, Daphne stammered to a halt, her words lost in an answering smile.

"No, it's perfect timing," Sparrow insisted, placing her hand on Daphne's arm. "I've been inside all day and you're right, it is a wonderful afternoon for a walk. If you don't mind waiting, I'll just change my blouse and put on my walking shoes."

"No rush, take your time," Daphne replied, taking a seat.

A few moments later, Sparrow rejoined her in the living room wearing a pair of lightweight, summer capri pants and a soft pink blouse. Feeling emboldened, she had also added a touch of lipstick and some perfume. Sparrow felt a ripple of happiness at the obvious appreciation on Daphne's face.

"I've got my keys and jacket, so let's go," she said softly.

Taking a deep breath as she got to her feet, Daphne followed her outside.

"Which way were you thinking of going?" Sparrow asked as she locked her front door.

"Well, I thought the lake walk would be nice. I saw some new ducklings there the other day and I thought we might visit them."

"That sounds perfect."

The sun had lowered enough to take the sting out of the heat, and the gentle breeze brought the scent of freshly mown grass. Sparrow took a deep breath, feeling the warmth resonate through her body.

"So, what brought you to OWL's Haven, Daphne?" she asked as they walked, eager to learn more about her suddenly reticent companion.

"Same thing as most of us, I guess," said Daphne. "I had been living on my own in Sydney for about five years and was thinking I should sell my house. Originally, I planned to sell it and just buy a smaller cottage. Then some Army buddies of mine, who had recently moved into a retirement village, dragged me along to an open day.

"I had always imagined they would be full of old people just sitting around waiting to die. However, when I saw the place for myself, I was pleasantly surprised. The people were friendly; the cottages were nice; it felt...I don't know... normal. I went home and thought about what I was going to do, but kept putting off the decision. Then, a few months later, I read an article in a magazine about OWL's Haven and came down to see it for myself." Daphne stopped and looked at the beautifully tended grounds surrounding them. "I was so impressed that I went back and had my house on the market by the end of that week. I've never regretted moving here; it's the best thing I've done in years."

Sparrow smiled, nodding in agreement. "Tell me about your years in the Army?" she asked, taking advantage of their burgeoning rapport by linking her arm through Daphne's. "What made you join up?"

Gently bringing Sparrow in closer, Daphne blew out a deep breath. "My father and I..." Daphne paused, her jaw clenching. "Well, I think the best thing I can say about him is that we didn't get along. He was basically a bully and a thug and usually took his anger out on my mother. I tried to protect her, but he'd wait until I'd left for school and she was alone." Swallowing hard, she continued. "She died when I was fifteen. The day of her funeral I thought my heart was going to break. After she died, he just moved his viciousness onto me. I loved school and loved learning, but once it was finished for the day I'd go anywhere but home."

Seeing Sparrow's look of distress, Daphne shrugged. "It was OK. I ended up spending a lot of time on the streets and got caught up with a pretty wild crowd. Inevitably, the law caught up with me and I came to the attention of a social worker named Marion Harmon. Luckily for me, she saw through my arrogance and anger and organised for me to join a program with other street kids who were living in similar situations." Daphne laughed, remembering. "I so didn't want to join in, and I gave that poor woman a huge amount of grief, but to her credit and my incredible luck, she persevered. Eventually, I gave up fighting because it was just too hard to maintain and once I did, I realised that the program wasn't so bad after all."

Sparrow squeezed Daphne's arm in silent encouragement and asked gently, "So you were living on the streets?"

"Well, I'd figured out I was a lesbian by then and the old man wouldn't have me in the house. I used to stay with mates when I could; otherwise I would sneak into the back shed and sleep there. One evening, when I was sixteen, an Army recruitment team came to give a talk to our youth group. Afterwards, I spoke to Marion about my interest in what the Army could offer me, so she organised with a friend of hers to give me a personal tour. I came home from that visit knowing that joining the Army was exactly what I wanted to do."

"But there was only one problem." Daphne's tone roughened, and Sparrow looked up, concern on her face. "My father had to sign the form for me to join. He refused, threatening to tell them I was a queer. We got into a fight and I punched him—knocked him clean off his feet."

Daphne stopped, looking down at Sparrow. "That sounds bad doesn't it?" she asked quietly, removing her arm from Sparrow's grip. "I was tall and pretty strong by then and it was as if every ounce of anger I had stored inside me just exploded. I said that if he didn't sign, I'd call the police and tell them who was responsible for the latest wave of burglaries going on in our neighbourhood."

"No," Sparrow said fiercely. "You did what you had to do." Leaning in, she took Daphne's hand and held it gently in her own. "So, what happened?"

"Well, it seemed to do the trick and the day after my seventeenth birthday, I joined the Army." Daphne kicked at a pebble. "He died soon after I enlisted. I didn't even bother going to the funeral. As far as I was concerned, it was a blessing. Besides, I had a new life and it was taking up all my time."

They resumed walking. "Was it as good as you had hoped?"

"Oh, you have no idea," Daphne said, a smile chasing away the sadness. "I remember when the bus dropped us all at the Recruit Training Centre in Mosman. I was terrified. It was the first time that I was completely in charge of my own life. I couldn't believe how much there was to learn. We seemed to spend all our time studying, cleaning and trying to stay out of the path of our instructors. They terrified us all into blind obedience. I remember meeting one of those instructors years later and she still made me nervous!"

Sparrow laughed at the exaggerated depiction.

"Still, once I had been there a while and started to relax, I came to love it. I was young, I had direction, purpose and order. And for the first time in several years, I was also safe, well fed and way too busy to worry about getting into trouble."

"So what exactly did you do in the Army?" Sparrow asked, brushing her hand against the lavender bushes that lined their walk.

Both women breathed in the scent as Daphne continued her story. "I started in driver training. It was terrific. I learnt how to drive all these amazing trucks. Because I was tall and fit, I was able to handle them quite easily. Then as I progressed through the ranks, I became an instructor myself."

"What was that like?" Sparrow asked, imagining a young Daphne in her Army greens.

Daphne shook her head. "Well, by the time I got promoted to that level I was well and truly ready for it, so it felt fine. However, it was just another part of my personal journey. Being an instructor taught me to lead, to take charge."

The thought caused Sparrow to break out in goosebumps. "Oh, how wonderful," she breathed, stumbling a little.

Daphne stopped. "Are you all right?" she asked, concerned. "Are you tired? Do you want to turn back?"

Sparrow gazed up at her. "No, I'm fine. Go on, you were…taking charge," she prompted with a smile.

Daphne tucked Sparrow's arm under hers once again. "Well, I guess the experience gave me a perspective I didn't even know I needed. Sometimes things happen in life for a reason. I have always believed that Marion and the Army saved my life. I hate to think what would have happened to me if I'd been left to just run wild. I probably would have been dead, or in jail, by the time I was twenty."

They arrived at the lake, and Daphne turned to Sparrow. "I don't know about you, but a bench seat under a tree has never looked so good."

Taking a handkerchief out of her pocket, Daphne quickly gave the bench a wipe over. As they sat and caught their breath, the sound of water birds feeding nearby created a relaxing backdrop.

"What about your love life; did you have a girlfriend in the Army?" Sparrow asked once they had settled.

Daphne blushed, carefully folding her handkerchief. "Well, of course in those days, you had to be so careful. Anyone caught 'fraternising' was kicked out immediately. However, I...managed. There was a sizeable group of us, and although it got a little incestuous at times, we did just fine," she said with a sly grin.

Sparrow chuckled. "So why did you leave?" she asked, turning to look at her companion.

"Well, I completed thirty years of service, and then finally decided I'd had enough. I had a pension from the Army and had met the woman of my dreams, who I thought I was going to spend the rest of my life with. I'd spent so many years hiding my relationships, and I just didn't want to do that anymore. The rules around homosexuality were much more relaxed by then and it wasn't such a big deal, but I was ready for something new. I was offered a wonderful job as the NSW state manager of the biggest vehicle service company in Australia and stayed with them until I retired, thirteen years later."

"And the woman of your dreams?" Sparrow asked gently.

"Well, let's just say that I wasn't what she wanted after all and leave it at that," Daphne replied lightly

Sparrow squeezed her hand. "I'm so sorry."

Daphne turned and looked down at her. Gently tucking a lock of hair behind Sparrow's ear, she smiled. "You know what? Right now, I'm not sorry at all. As I said earlier, I truly believe that things happen for a reason."

At that moment, a mother duck with four ducklings in tow swam noisily across the lake, drawing their attention. They watched in delight as she shepherded her charges into the thick reeds, where they would be safe from any predators.

"Well they're all tucked in for the night," observed Sparrow, glancing at her watch, "and we had better be getting back before it gets dark."

Rising, the women began the walk back arm in arm, their conversation sporadic but relaxed. When they arrived at her cottage, Sparrow turned and looked up at Daphne.

"Would you like to come in for a cup of coffee?" she asked as she opened her front door.

Daphne hesitated, biting her lip and looking at her watch, and Sparrow felt their newfound intimacy dissipate.

"Would you mind if I take a rain check?" she asked hesitantly.

"Not at all," Sparrow said, smiling to hide her disappointment. "Thank you so much for the walk. I really enjoyed getting to know a little more about you and your life."

"We seemed to spend a lot of time talking about my life, so I hope I didn't bore you too much," Daphne replied tentatively.

Taking Daphne's hand, Sparrow stood up on her tiptoes to place a gentle kiss on her cheek.

"Of course not," she whispered.

They stood silently looking at each other for a long moment, until Daphne finally started to move away. "You have a good night, Sparrow. Thanks again for the walk," she called softly, with a wave.

Sparrow stood and watched her leave, then slowly closed her front door.

Chapter 8

ALLIE BALANCED THE FOOD CONTAINERS on her hip as she knocked on the door of the cottage. The staff had organised a day trip to the beach with a barbeque lunch for the residents, and despite Pat's reluctance, Allie had persuaded her to go with them, offering to spend the day with Bella.

When she opened the door, Pat gave Allie a kiss on the cheek before taking the containers from her.

"Are you sure you are happy to do this, Allie? I don't mind not going, you know."

Allie followed Pat through to the kitchen and watched as she put the food in the refrigerator. Pat's large frame seemed to have shrunk over the last eight weeks; she looked exhausted.

Smiling encouragingly, Allie took her friend's hand. "No backing out now, madam. Besides, I've never been much of a beach girl and this will give us both a wonderful chance to catch up."

Pat squeezed Allie's hand. "Honestly, she has been feeling so sick lately that I've been turning visitors away, but she has been looking forward to your visit so much. I'll just go and let her know you're here."

Allie wandered into the living room. A comfortable sofa with a hand crocheted rug folded on one of the arms sat in shafts of sunshine streaming through the window. Allie ran her hands across the top of the two well-used recliner chairs strategically placed in front of a wide screen television with the obligatory cable box on top. Like all the cottages, Pat and Bella's living room had large windows overlooking a compact courtyard and garden, sunlight ensuring the space was cosy and inviting. Through the archway was a small dining room with a table and chairs. Bella's artwork hung on the walls throughout the cottage, and Allie noticed sadly that there appeared to be no new paintings since she had last visited. A large bookcase took up one wall and framed pictures of the couple were scattered on every surface. Walking over for a closer look, Allie picked up a photo that she hadn't seen before. Bella and Pat were standing in front of a fountain with their arms around each other, laughing into the camera.

Pat walked up behind her. "That was taken about twelve years ago when we decided we needed to visit Rome. Bella had heard so much about it over the years, from her family, but had never been, so we saved up and spent two months over there. That was taken just before we left. We had just thrown coins into the Trevi Fountain and made our wish. It was such a great holiday."

Allie placed the photo gently back on the shelf, both of them suddenly at a loss for words.

"I'm not sure if Bella is eating much, but I have some chicken soup I made and I put a little rice with it. I thought if I brought it, I might be able to persuade her to share it with me," Allie said, breaking the moment.

Pat smiled. "Well, she does love your chicken soup, and anything you can get her to eat would be wonderful. Her appetite comes and goes, so I would definitely give it a try."

"Why don't you get yourself ready? I think the bus is picking everyone up in about ten minutes at the office."

Pat nodded. "Bella's in the bedroom. Go right in, she's expecting you."

Allie walked through to the bedroom and as she caught sight of Bella, her heart constricted. When had she gotten so thin and frail?

Bella beamed at her, and Allie was reminded how her smile could light up a room.

"Allie," Bella held out both hands in greeting.

Allie took them, and kissed her on each cheek. "Hello, Bella, how..." Allie stopped suddenly, realising what a ridiculous question she was about to ask.

Laughing, Bella patted the bed next to her for Allie to sit down. "It's fine, you know—you can ask how I am."

Allie blushed. "I'm sorry. I feel like an idiot."

At that moment, Pat walked in. "I'm off, ladies. Is there anything you need before I go?"

Bella smiled. "No, darling. Go and have a good time and don't worry about me. Have you got a hat and sunscreen?"

Pat took the tube of sunscreen and hat out of her tote bag. "Yes, and a bottle of water."

"Excellent, then give me a kiss and go, before you miss the pick-up."

Pat leant over and placed a gentle kiss on Bella's forehead. "Don't get up to too much mischief while I'm gone."

"I'll see you out," offered Allie. "Bella, I'll be back in a minute."

At the front door, Pat turned to her. "If anything happens, the emergency numbers are on the fridge. I've got my mobile with me, and the nurse will be here around four this afternoon to give her a shower. Hopefully, I'll be back before then, but…"

Allie gave her a hug. "Pat, she'll be fine, I promise. Try to make today about you. I've got Bella, so go and kick your heels up with the others."

Pat hugged her hard. "Thanks, Allie. I'll see you when I get back."

Allie watched as Pat made her way down the pathway to meet the bus. Closing the door, she took a deep breath and walked back to the bedroom.

<hr />

Bella wanted to sit in the courtyard, so after gathering the necessary blankets and pillows, Allie helped her to her feet. With Bella leaning on Allie's arm, they moved slowly outside.

"Now, if you could move that sunbed under the pergola, that would be perfect," Bella said, sitting in a chair to catch her breath.

Allie moved the furniture, arranged the rugs and got Bella settled. She moved a small table nearer to Bella, then went to the kitchen for a carafe of water and glasses, which she placed within Bella's reach.

Bella put her face up to catch the rays of sun filtering through the grapevine covering the patio. "Oh, this is just what I needed," she said softly. "Thank you, Allie."

Settling herself in a chair across from Bella, Allie poured them each a water.

"So, tell me, what's been happening in the village? Pat and I have missed out on so much and I want to hear all the gossip," Bella declared, taking a glass.

Allie soon had Bella laughing gleefully over her detailed description of the late-night swim and the Tupperware presentation.

"I wish I'd been there to see Leslie at the Tupperware presentation," Bella chuckled, dabbing at her tears of laughter.

"Oh yes, it was one of her better moments. Of course, thanks to Meg plying me with alcohol, I barely remember any of it! I only have Meg's version to rely on, and we all know that she never lets truth stand in the way of a good story," Allie said with a roll of her eyes.

"What about Daphne and Sparrow? Do you think there's a chance of a romance happening with them?" Bella asked.

"Well, I haven't seen much of them since that late-night swim, so I'm not sure. They are both on the trip today, so I shall ask Meg to give me all the details when she gets back this evening."

"Well, I hope they explore the possibilities," Bella said with a smile. "From what you say, she seems the type of woman who might just be able to get through Daphne's defences."

With a sigh, Bella leant back in her chair and began picking at the corner of her rug. "I'm so glad Pat agreed to go on this trip today. She so needs a break—and just between us, so do I."

Allie regarded her friend quizzically.

Bella stopped fiddling and smoothed the rug over her legs, choosing her words with care. "I love her so much, but there are times when I desperately need to be by myself. I look at her and see how much pain this is all causing her. She is so exhausted from dealing with the stress and looking after me, and I find myself..." Bella stopped and bit her lip.

Allie leant in and took her hand. "It's all right. You can tell me, Bella."

Tears filled Bella's eyes as she squeezed Allie's hand.

"I feel so awful, but there are times when I just want to shout and scream. I want to howl at the moon because this is all so unfair. I get so incredibly angry and all I can do is lash out at Pat. But then I see the distress in her eyes and I stop myself, because I don't want to cause her any more pain. Pat was so against me going through the chemo in the first place, which makes me feel even more selfish. But the feelings don't go away, Allie, and I don't know how to deal with them." Bella lay her head back, exhausted by her emotional outburst.

Allie stroked Bella's hand, concern evident on her face. "Have you talked to anyone at the hospital about this?" she asked gently.

"No. I feel so ungrateful, and I keep telling myself that I just have to deal with it. I have tried to talk to her, but what do I say? How do I explain it all to her, without her being incredibly hurt?" Bella asked. "She's trying so hard to protect me, but I don't want to be protected. I need to be able to be angry and sad and cry and throw things, and not worry about how Pat is going to deal with it. Did you know the hospital wanted to admit me as a patient for this round of chemo?"

Allie's eyes widened. "No! Why did they want to do that?"

"They were worried about how sick this treatment was making me. Anyway, Louise, bless her, decided that it would be too stressful for me to be away from Pat, so she organised for me to have a nurse at home. I know she meant it with the best intentions, and Pat was thrilled, but there have been times, Allie, when I've wished I was in that hospital and away from her, just for a couple of days. Even getting her to go out today was a huge effort."

Squeezing Allie's hand, she smiled. "You have no idea how much I've been looking forward to us just spending this afternoon together. Then last night, Pat announced that she had changed her mind and decided she wouldn't be going on the trip today. We came as close to a fight as we have in ages. I wanted to have a true Italian tantrum, but she backed off and it all got pushed under the carpet…again."

Allie stroked her hand. "Oh, Bella, I'm so incredibly sorry."

Bella took a tissue from her pocket and wiped her eyes. "I honestly didn't mean to unload all this on you, but it's so good just to be able to talk about it."

"Don't be silly. I feel terrible that I haven't been around more often. Maybe I could have helped with all this."

"That's what I mean. I know I have been feeling awful and with the chemo there was initially a quarantine period, but people have been to see me and Pat has turned them away. She doesn't seem to understand that I need to keep in touch with all of you. I want to know what's going on around me, or, at least, to be given that option. We can't be everything to each other, Allie. It's not fair on either of us. But I'm not being given that choice, which just makes it all that much harder."

"Well, what we need to do is work out how we can change the situation," Allie offered. "Pat obviously needs to know all this, but we have to find a way of telling her without her feeling betrayed or hurt. How do you feel about the two of you talking to a counsellor at the hospital? They must deal with this issue all the time."

Bella looked thoughtful. "Well, I have spoken briefly to the social worker there. Louise set up an appointment for me when I started this last round of treatment. I could ask her about setting up a meeting with the counsellor. But what do I tell Pat?"

"Well, firstly, I think you should have a meeting with a counsellor by yourself and fill them in on your situation. Tell them what you've told me and ask their advice. You can't keep going on like this. You need to put all your energy into getting yourself well."

"Believe me, the irony is not lost on me," Bella replied with a shrug. "Give me a couple of days to think about it. I am due back at the hospital next Thursday, so I might make a phone call before then to organise an appointment." A worried expression crossed Bella's face. "What will I tell Pat, though? She'll think I am trying to hide something from her if I say I want to talk to someone by myself."

"Leave that with me. I'll find a way to keep Pat here for the day and give you some time alone with the hospital staff."

Bella squeezed Allie's hand. "You have no idea how much better I feel having talked all this through with you. At least now it feels as if I'm not dealing with this all on my own."

"You know it will probably also help Pat to sit down and talk to a counsellor. She has to be finding this situation just as hard as you are. Is there anyone that you know of that she has been talking to about her feelings?" Allie asked.

Bella sighed. "No, she's fairly private. It's so hard to get her to talk about feelings and emotions, even with me. It's much easier for me. I can talk about feelings for hours." She gave a small laugh. "But I think Pat has been keeping it all locked up inside. I was hoping she might have talked to Daphne, as they have always been close. But Pat hasn't mentioned anything about Daphne and Sparrow, so it's possible that they haven't really spoken in a while, and that concerns me. I know Daphne has called her several times and invited her over, but Pat's put her off. I'm sure Daphne is wondering what's going on."

Allie agreed. "I'll talk to Daphne and see if she can get Pat over to her place for a football night. Once you've finished the meeting with the counsellor, we can organise a roster. That way, when you feel up to it, a few of us can come over and sit with you, and Pat can have some time off for herself."

"I don't know why I didn't talk to you about this weeks ago." Bella smiled. "I can't believe there may be such a simple solution."

"Well, we aren't out of the woods yet, but, as my mother used to say, I think we might have found the path. I'm glad I'm able to help. Just let me know what you need and if I can help in any way, you know I will. And now," Allie declared, standing up and stretching, "I don't know about you, but I'm hungry. I brought some of my chicken soup that you like so much. If I heat it up, do you think you would be able to join me in a small bowl?"

"You brought your homemade chicken soup?" Bella asked, her eyes lighting up.

"None other, madam, especially for you, and just for a change, I added a little rice."

"Mmm, just what I feel like," said Bella.

"You sit tight and I'll go heat it up. Do you need anything else while I'm in the kitchen?"

"No, nothing I can think of."

"Well, you just lie back and relax and a bowl of soup will be here in a flash," Allie said, tucking the blanket snugly around Bella's legs.

In the kitchen, Allie set to work preparing their meal. One of the things she and Bella shared was their love of food. The two of them had spent many happy afternoons messing about in each other's kitchens, experimenting with recipes and testing new dishes.

Taking the tray of food through, she deposited two small bowls of delicious smelling broth on the table. She handed one to Bella with a napkin, then took her own bowl from the tray and sat down in the chair next to her.

Bella raised her water glass. "*Buon Appetito*."

Allie clinked her glass against Bella's. "*Buon Appetito* to you too, my friend. I hope you enjoy it."

"It smells heavenly. Is that fresh coriander?" asked Bella.

"Just a touch. I thought it would add to the flavour. I know how much you love it."

For the next five minutes the only sounds were spoons clinking against bowls. Watching Bella out of the corner of her eye, Allie was pleased to see that she was tucking into the soup with great relish. Before long both bowls were empty.

"Oh that was wonderful," Bella sighed contentedly.

"There's more if you want."

Bella held up her hand. "No, that amount was just perfect."

"I'll leave the rest in the container in the fridge in case you feel like some later on. Do you want anything else?"

Bella yawned. "No, I feel so much better after that meal."

Bella's colour was improving and although she was obviously still tired, Allie thought she seemed more relaxed.

"Well, why don't you have a nap while I fix these dishes? Then I can sit and read. You two have made a perfect little nook out here," she observed, looking around.

Bella smiled. "I can't believe these vines grew so fast. We only put them in about five years ago, but you are right. They make this patio the perfect spot for a lazy afternoon snooze."

"Are you warm enough? You aren't in a draft are you?" Allie asked.

"No, it's all just perfect. Thank you so much, Allie." Bella yawned again, her eyes slowly closing.

Dropping a soft kiss on her cheek, Allie collected the tray and left Bella to her nap.

Chapter 9

PAT WATCHED FROM HER SEAT as the other OWL's day-trippers boarded the bus. Winter seemed to have flown by and the warm sunny day hinted that summer was only around the corner. As the women clambered aboard, Pat smiled at the variety of white winter legs clad in the first shorts of the season.

"Hey Pat! I didn't know you were coming," Daphne called as she made her way down the aisle, a huge smile on her expressive face. She, together with a small woman Pat had not previously seen, settled in the two seats across the aisle.

Daphne leant over to Pat. "How's Bella coping with the chemo?" she asked quietly.

Pat shrugged. "She has good days and bad days. She's spending the afternoon with Allie, which will cheer her up."

Squeezing her arm in sympathy, Daphne gestured to her companion. "By the way, I am not sure if you have met Sparrow?"

Pat leant forward, nodding at the other woman. "No, I don't believe we have met."

Sparrow smiled. "It's lovely to finally meet you."

Several other women stopped to say hello to Pat on their way to taking a seat. When Meg reached them, she greeted her with characteristic acerbity, "Well, it's about time you joined the rest of us. Some of us were seriously starting to worry about you."

Daphne coughed and nudged Meg. "I think what Meg meant to say," she said pointedly, "is that it's great to see you again."

Meg cast Daphne a steely look and raised her eyebrow. Giving Pat a squeeze on the shoulder, she moved past, heading to the back of the bus.

Leslie, who was coming up the aisle behind Meg, broke into a grin when she saw Pat.

"Well, hello Pat, what a wonderful surprise! I haven't seen you in ages. Do you mind if I sit next to you?" Leslie indicated the spare seat.

"Hey, Leslie, it's nice to see you too. No, the seat is empty, help yourself." Pat stepped into the aisle so Leslie could slide past.

Once everyone was on board and settled, Pat watched as the driver walked down the bus checking the names off her clipboard.

"Now, ladies, you know the drill, seatbelts on—and keep them on," she reiterated firmly, casting a look at Meg and several others at the back of the bus.

Pat smiled as Meg rolled her eyes, displaying her fastened seat belt to the driver

"Great to see you are all in top form today," the driver declared with a smile, moving back towards the front of the bus. "Now if you are all ready and your seatbelts are on, we'll be on our way."

The bus rumbled to life and Pat sat back, listening to the chatter around her. Despite her reluctance to leave Bella, she found herself caught up in the general good humour, and realised how much she was looking forward to the prospect of a day with her friends.

Pat watched Sparrow and Daphne, their heads close together, talking quietly. As Sparrow took Daphne's hand, Pat was shocked to realise just how much she had missed over the last several weeks. She glanced over at Leslie, who was scrolling through her iPad.

"I see you've got one of those things as well," Pat said. "Bella and I were talking about them the other day."

"This?" Leslie indicated the device. "Oh, Pat, it's the most wonderful toy. My grandson introduced me to it."

"So, basically, it's like having a miniature portable computer?" Pat asked.

Leslie nodded. "Exactly. I mean, it has some limitations, but one of the reasons I love it so much is that it gives me instant, twenty-four-hour access to all the newspapers and news sites. I've got it all on here, from ABC to CNN, as well as *The New York Times*, *The Australian* and *The Times*."

"I'm not a great computer whiz, but Bella loves them, and apparently these iPads have wonderful art doodads... I can't remember what they are called." Pat laughed.

"Apps," Leslie supplied.

Pat nodded. "That's it. Well, I thought because they are so portable, it would be a terrific idea for Bella so she can keep doing her art, even if she's in bed. I know she misses painting, but she just doesn't have the energy right now. This might be just what she needs. Do you know anything about the art apps?"

Sparrow leant in to Daphne. "How long have Pat and Bella been together?"

"Forty-five years," she answered with a sigh.

Sparrow grimaced. "Oh, that has to be hard for them. The cancer."

Daphne nodded. "Between you and me, I don't think it's a promising outcome, but we are all keeping our fingers crossed."

Sparrow sat quietly, watching Pat and wondering at the turmoil she must be experiencing. After several moments, she gently reached out for Daphne's hand.

"I guess you never know what's around the corner."

Looking down at their joined hands, Daphne smiled. "No, I guess you never do," she replied softly, linking her fingers through Sparrow's.

———— ⟨✦⟩ ————

Pat felt the excitement growing as the bus started winding its way down the road leading to their destination. Gazing through the window, she smiled at the sight of the horseshoe bay ringed with white sand. The ocean was calm, waves lapping the shore softly. She watched as the gulls effortlessly rode the air currents, soaring and dipping over the sparkling water, the noise of their calls echoing around the bay.

As the bus stopped, she rose and stretched. Grabbing her bag, she moved towards the exit, greeting friends as she went. She was standing by the picnic tables looking out at the ocean when she felt a tap on her shoulder.

"Fancy a walk down the beach?" Daphne asked.

"Sure, if you have nothing else planned," Pat replied, indicating Sparrow chatting to several other women.

"It's fine; walk with me and tell me what's been going on with you. I haven't seen you in weeks." Kicking off her sandals, Daphne began trudging through the sand, away from the others.

Pat sighed as she joined her, relishing the feel of the warm sand between her toes. "Same old, same old, I guess."

Daphne stopped. "Pat Campbell, you are not being straight with me. Now I want to know why you haven't been returning my calls and why you've been avoiding all of us. Meg's right, you know, you've just completely dropped out of sight."

"Oh, sorry," Pat said snidely, "didn't you hear? My partner's got cancer and I have rather a lot on my plate right now."

Both women were shocked into silence.

Horrified at her outburst, Pat closed her eyes, misery etched on her face. "Oh shit, Daphne, I am so sorry. I didn't mean that!"

Daphne put her arms around Pat as she started to cry.

"Hey, it's all right," she crooned, holding the shaking woman tight.

"No, it's not," Pat exclaimed angrily, pulling away. "It's a lot of bloody things, but all right is not one of them. I'm fucking falling apart, and I don't know what to do."

Daphne took her arm, and Pat followed her over to a depression in a small sand dune where they could sit in privacy. Pat took a tissue from her pocket and dabbed at her eyes.

Sitting close, Daphne looked carefully at her. "Talk to me. Tell me what's happening."

Pat sat shredding her tissue, tears falling freely. "I just don't know how much longer I can hang on. Some days Bella won't even talk to me, and I don't know what to do. We don't know if this treatment is working, but she insists on carrying it through to the end. I feel like I'm just watching her slip away and am powerless to do anything about it." Pat mopped frantically at her tears. "I'm terrified to leave her in case something happens while I'm away. I know it drives her crazy, but I can't help it. Last night she became so incredibly angry when I mentioned I might not come on today's trip. I swear it was as if she hated me."

Pat looked across at her friend, her expression desperate. "I can't lose her, Daphne. She is the only woman I have ever loved. When I met her, I was eighteen, six feet tall and a hundred and sixty-eight pounds. I stuck out like a sore thumb; I felt like a freak. I was so shy I could barely say hello to most people, and I was just so miserable. None of that mattered to Bella, though; she treated me like I was the most gorgeous woman on earth. I couldn't believe that this truly beautiful, gentle woman wanted nothing more than to be with me; it was as if a door had been unlocked. In all the years we have been together, we have been able to talk about anything, even through her first bout with cancer, but now I can't seem to say anything..." Pat stopped, choked with emotion.

"Go on," Daphne gently prodded after a moment.

Pat ran her hand roughly over her face. "Isn't that enough?"

"No, there's more. Come on, let it all out and then we can talk about it."

"When did you suddenly become Dr Daphne?" Pat muttered with a ghost of a smile.

Daphne bumped her shoulder. "Quit stalling."

Pat took a deep breath. "Bella was so excited that Allie was coming around today…"

Daphne waited.

"…well it sounds so stupid but I realised I was jealous that she wanted to spend time with Allie, rather than me." Pat buried her face in her hands.

Daphne sat quietly staring out at the ocean, her face a study in concentration. After a while, she put her arm around Pat and spoke quietly.

"I don't know much about a lot of stuff. I left school at seventeen and joined the Army, so I'm not that academically inclined, but I have had a few relationships in my life and there's one thing I can tell you with certainty. Apart from infidelity, there is almost nothing that can't be fixed by two people talking. I can't begin to imagine what you two have been through with these two bouts of cancer, but I do know that you've had a lifetime of experiences to get you through it." Turning, she made eye contact with Pat. "You and Bella have got to talk about all this. Right now it sounds like the two of you are coping with this alone, when you should be coping with it together."

"I don't know what to say to her," Pat confessed miserably, looking out at the ocean.

"Then let her talk and you listen to what she says. You know Bella, she loves talking about feelings and all that stuff. You and me, we aren't so good at that."

Pat nodded. "You got that right."

"Give her some time and space every now and then. Come over to my place, watch some football and have some beers, just like we used to. Give Bella the chance to have some of her friends over, or just spend some time alone. If she's too sick for visitors, she'll tell them. You just have to love her; you don't have to manage her."

Pat dropped her head on her arms and let out a big sigh. Daphne gently rubbed her back.

"You can always come and play a game of golf with me."

Puzzled, Pat lifted her head, frowning. "You don't play golf."

"I know, that way you can always be guaranteed of winning," Daphne replied with a grin. "Greater love hath no woman for her friend than to play golf with her, knowing she is going to get thrashed."

Pat chuckled. "Thanks Daph." Sifting the sand through her fingers, she shook her head. "I know you're right, it's just been so damned hard."

"Of course it has, but I've missed our time together. It hasn't been the same without you cluttering up my living room and drinking all my beer."

"I've missed you too. I just haven't been very good company lately," she admitted sadly.

"Hey, you and Bella have always been there for me, even when I didn't realise I needed you. Let me help you with this. What is it you two are always telling me? You don't have to do it alone."

Pat gave a shy smile, fighting back more tears. "Thanks, buddy," she said hoarsely.

"And trust me, if you don't, I'll come around and drag you over to my place, kicking and screaming," Daphne warned.

Pat held up her hands in mock surrender. "I promise, whatever you say."

Staring out at the ocean, Pat let the rhythm of the waves slowly calm her. Taking a deep breath, she turned to Daphne. "So, do you feel ready to go and see if there is anything left of the barbeque?"

Daphne held out her hand. "Only if you pull me up. I think my legs have seized up on me."

Standing and dusting the sand from her pants, Pat laughed. She grabbed Daphne's hand and pulled her to her feet. "Just remember, you're the younger one, so you can't play the old lady card. Come on, you old bag of bones."

Together they walked slowly back towards the scattered group at the picnic area.

"So, is it my imagination, or is there something going on with you and Sparrow?" Pat asked.

Daphne suddenly became fascinated with something out at sea. "Well, um…I'm not, um, sure at this stage, maybe…" she stuttered, reddening with embarrassment.

Pat laughed at her friend's obvious discomfort. "That's great. She seems nice. I mean, not that I've gotten to talk to her much, but she seems to like you and that's always a good start."

"Yeah, well, we are just taking things slowly. You know how it is, the village is a hive of gossip, and we want to keep things quiet until we figure out where we want to go with this."

"So you haven't…" Pat tapered off with a smile, wriggling her eyebrows.

"Oh hell's teeth, Pat!" Daphne slapped her arm.

"Well, I was just asking."

Daphne coloured once more. "Well, not that it is anyone's business, but no, we haven't…you know. We thought we'd wait," she mumbled.

Pat frowned in confusion. "Wait? What for? It's not as if you aren't old enough, or…she has had sex before, hasn't she?" Pat asked in mock horror.

Daphne kicked sand at her. "Of course she has, you great goof. I don't know, it was Sparrow's idea and I just agreed. I mean, it makes sense, doesn't it? We don't want to rush into anything, and I can't remember the last time I had sex, so I need a bit of time to get used to that idea again. The truth is, I'm torn between desperately wanting to see her naked again and feeling terrified at the thought of what happens next."

Pat stopped in her tracks, staring at Daphne in puzzlement. "What do you mean, again? I thought you said you hadn't had sex; when exactly did you see her naked?"

Daphne turned. "Oh, Lord, don't tell me you haven't heard about the late-night skinny dip?"

"The what?" Pat spluttered.

Daphne laughed. "Oh, you're going to love this story." Between bouts of raucous laughter, she filled Pat in.

Pat shook her head. "Oh, I wish I'd been there for that," she laughed. "You've got to hand it to Meg, she sure can come up with some loony ideas. So you just lifted this woman right out of the water, hey? It's a wonder you didn't have a stroke next to all that naked flesh."

Daphne rolled her eyes "Oh, you have no idea. She's so tiny, I had to lift her up quite high, and her backside was suddenly right there in front of me. It took all my self-control not to take a bite."

"Eeww…too much information there, mate," Pat hooted, screwing up her face.

"Well, you asked." Daphne smirked.

"Well, for what it's worth, I think you should just go for it. You're not getting any younger, you know. You'd hate to wait so long that you got Alzheimer's and forgot what it was you had to do."

"Oh, don't worry, I get the feeling that Sparrow would remind me." Daphne laughed again.

"Speaking of whom…" Pat gestured at the woman coming towards them.

"Oh there you are," called Sparrow. "I was just coming to look for you. The barbecue's ready and we better be quick or we'll miss out."

Daphne clapped Pat on the back. "Well then, my friend, let's go eat."

Chapter 10

As ALLIE DROVE INTO HER carport, she noticed Meg about to enter her front door. Giving a quick toot of her horn, she waved. After gathering her things and locking the car, she waited as Meg hurried over to join her.

"Hey there." Allie smiled at Meg's windswept appearance. "How was the beach?"

"Terrific!" Meg replied. "I probably got too much sun, and I've got sand in places I don't even want to think about, but it was just what I needed to blow the cobwebs away."

Delighted by Meg's ebullient mood, Allie grinned. "A glass of wine to celebrate then?"

"You read my mind."

In the cottage, both women dropped their bags on the hall table and walked through into the kitchen.

"So, how was your day with Bella?" Meg asked.

"Interesting," Allie replied, nodding thoughtfully.

Opening the fridge, she took out a bottle of wine and homemade cheese sticks. Meg collected two glasses from the shelf, followed her into the living room and dropped with a heartfelt sigh onto the sofa.

They toasted each other, and Meg savoured the wine. "Oh, that's heavenly." Taking a deep breath, she turned to face Allie. "So, tell me what's happening with Bella."

Allie gently twirled the stem of her wine glass. "They've got bigger problems than just Bella's illness right now. You were right, you know; she is feeling totally smothered by Pat and it's causing some serious issues for them. We talked about it for over an hour; she's almost at her wits' end."

Meg sighed, bringing the bowl of cheese sticks between them on the sofa and picking one up. "Well, I'm not surprised," she said, taking a bite. "You and I both know that Pat's become almost obsessive with Bella since she got this second diagnosis. So, did you come up with a solution?"

"Well, once she let it all out, we decided that she needed professional help. She knows she has to be honest with Pat, but is worried that she'll be incredibly hurt and the whole situation will just end up being worse than it already is. She needs professional advice on how to avoid that." Allie placed her hand on Meg's arm. "Oh, I nearly forgot. I've also promised to organise a roster of visitors for her, so she feels less isolated from what's happening around her. I know she's not well, but I think she would genuinely enjoy a small group of us visiting her at home in her off-chemo weeks. If nothing else, it'll help lift her spirits. The other thing we need to do is organise for Pat to talk to someone as well, because this has to be causing huge emotional problems for her."

Meg nodded, licking the crumbs from her fingers. "I think all those are great ideas. Interestingly, Pat and Daphne went off for a walk this afternoon and were gone quite a long time. When they got back, I'm sure Pat had been crying, so maybe that process has already begun."

"Well, I thought I might have a chat with Daphne tomorrow and just give her a head's up, see if she can help."

The two sat companionably drinking their wine, and Meg soon had Allie laughing as she related titbits from the day's outing.

"So, is there any further progress on the Daphne-Sparrow romance?" Allie asked, topping up their glasses.

"There is definitely something brewing there, but I get the impression they are trying to keep it under the radar. Not that I blame them; they would be totally in the spotlight. There are some women here that feed off that sort of gossip..." Meg said with a shudder, taking another cheese stick.

"Well, I for one hope they sort it out," Allie said. "They are two lovely women and although I don't know Sparrow that well, I can say for sure that it would be nice to see Daphne find someone."

"But don't you think they are..." Meg trailed off, waving her cheese stick in Allie's direction.

"What?" Allie asked, puzzled.

"Oh, I don't know. Total opposites, I guess. I mean, look at them. Daphne has to be close to six foot and Sparrow's lucky if she's five. I hate to be stating the obvious here, but could you find two women more physically different?"

"What, just because of their height?"

"Not just that. Daphne likes cars and beer and football and Sparrow... Well, Sparrow does embroidery, for Chrissake. I mean...come on." Meg laughed. "It's like the whole butch-femme stereotype playing out before our very eyes."

Allie laughed too. "I agree, but look at you and me."

Meg turned slowly to look at her. "What do you mean?" she asked uncertainly.

"Well, you couldn't find two more different people than the two of us, but look how close we are. Sometimes, I swear you know what I'm thinking before I do." Allie shrugged. "Anyway, I just think it's great that, at their age, they're brave enough to take a chance, and I hope they find the happiness they deserve."

Meg leant into Allie and put her head on her friend's shoulder. "You're a good woman, Allie Richards," she said softly.

Allie smiled as she leant her head against Meg's. "What makes you say that?"

Meg sat up and faced her. Reaching her hand over, she gently took a lock of Allie's hair and ran it through her fingers.

"Because you're kind and always want the best for everyone. You are a natural carer in a way I could never be." Cupping Allie's face in her hand, she leant in and placed a kiss on her cheek. "There's so much to love about you, and I'm so lucky to have had you in my life for so many years."

Allie took Meg's hand, unable to break eye contact. Meg was so close, she could feel her breath and it felt like the most natural thing in the world to lean in...

At the sound of Meg's ringtone from the hallway, they abruptly pulled apart.

Shocked, Allie picked up her wine glass and took a large swallow. She wasn't quite sure what the hell had just happened. She'd nearly kissed her best friend; more importantly, she'd *wanted* to kiss her best friend. Mortified and unable to look at Meg, Allie let out a breath as the phone finally went to message bank.

As they sat, the silence growing more awkward by the moment, so many thoughts went through Allie's mind, but she found herself unable to voice any of them. Meg just kept staring into her now empty wine glass.

"Well," said Meg finally, carefully placing her glass on the table and standing. "I suppose I should really get home. It's been a long day."

Allie rose as Meg walked to the hallway to collect her things. "It's only just six p.m. Are you sure you don't want to stay? I can whip us up a steak and salad," she offered hesitantly.

Meg gave a brief smile. "No, I'm for a shower and my bed. Thanks for the wine and…talk."

Allie followed Meg to the front door. Opening it, Meg turned to her.

"Sleep well, darling," she said lightly, cupping Allie's cheek in her hand. "We'll catch up tomorrow."

Allie watched until Meg entered her own cottage, then closed her front door, slowly returned to the living room and picked up the two wine glasses. In the kitchen, she emptied the contents of her glass into the sink before putting them both in the dishwasher. Emotions were bouncing inside her like a ping pong ball, and Allie felt completely incapable of dealing with any of it. Maybe she should just follow Meg's lead and sleep. With luck, tomorrow the two of them could just laugh it off and pretend nothing had ever happened.

Chapter 11

THE GAMES ROOM REVERBERATED WITH sounds of laughter. The monthly OWL's Haven poker game was in full swing; five women sat around a card table studying the cards Daphne had just dealt.

"Damn, Daphne!" Pat threw her hand on the table in disgust. "You have to be the worst dealer I've ever met."

Sporting the green eyeshade that she insisted on wearing at each game, Daphne did her best Chicago gangster impression. "If ya don't like the heat, honey, stay outta the kitchen."

Meg looked at Pat's dwindling pile of chips and laughed. "Stay out of the kitchen? I think she needs to stay out of the damned house!"

Challenging Pat to raise her stake, Daphne settled back in her chair.

Allie shuffled her cards around, trying to get a feel for the strength of the other players' hands. No matter how many times Meg reminded her that the poker game was just for fun, Allie's competitive spirit always put an extra edge to her tactics. Of all the regular players, Allie found Daphne the hardest to read. Over the months, she had quietly worked out all their various tell signs. Meg rubbed her ear, or played with her hair; Sparrow drummed her fingers; and Pat, the great goof, actually smiled when she was dealt a good hand. Daphne, however, had the consummate poker face and gave nothing away, a lesson Allie had learnt at great cost on the many occasions she had unsuccessfully challenged her.

As more players folded, it was deadlocked amongst Allie, Daphne and Meg. Allie's hand wasn't great: two pairs, kings and eights. Meg raised an eyebrow, running her hand through her hair. Eyeing the large pile of chips in the centre of the table, Allie was torn.

"I hate to rush you, but we aren't getting any younger here and I would like to finish this hand before my next birthday," Daphne said, glaring at Allie over the top of her glasses.

Allie narrowed her eyes, then took up the challenge. "All right, I'll see you," she announced decisively, moving her chips to the centre of the table

Meg nodded her agreement, and Daphne placed her hand face up on the table.

"Two pairs, aces and kings," she announced.

Allie groaned and tossed her hand on the table. "Damn, too good for me, kings and eights."

Meg smirked at Daphne. "Hmmm, pretty good hand," she acknowledged, still holding her cards close.

Daphne raised an eyebrow at Meg's teasing tone. "And what might you have cradled to that oh so attractive bosom of yours, pretty lady?"

The women around the table laughed as Meg shook her head. "I do so hate to disappoint a card shark such as yourself, but I think you may have just been beaten." With that, Meg laid down her hand and declared triumphantly, "My three twos beat your two pair."

Allie stared in amazement. "Three twos?" she asked. "You bet all those chips on three lousy twos?"

Meg let out a rare whoop of delight. "Well, I won, didn't I?" she gloated, sliding the chips from the centre of the table into her collection.

"By the way," Daphne said, as the next hand was being dealt, "is anyone going to Sydney for the Mardi Gras parade next March?"

"I was thinking about it," Sparrow replied, looking around at the group. "Anyone want to join me?"

Pat frowned at her cards. She wasn't much of a poker player, but Daphne had insisted she come to give herself a few hours away from caring for Bella.

"I haven't been for a few years, but Bella and I had a ball the last time we went."

"We should all go," Allie declared. "Just imagine all of us oldies marching. It would be fantastic. We could set up a senior lesbians contingent and teach those young ones a thing or two."

"It's a hell of a long walk. Maybe we could catch a lift with the Dykes on Bikes," Daphne suggested, winking at Sparrow.

Pat slapped the table. "I've got an even better idea. Why don't we each get one of those Vespa scooters that are all the rage? We could sail up Oxford Street on our little step-throughs, breasts bared to the wind. We'd be the 'Hooters on Scooters'. They'd all have to be lavender, of course!"

The women erupted in laughter.

"Now there's a truly terrifying picture," Meg chuckled. "The thought of you with no shirt on might send the crowd running."

Daphne grinned at Pat. "Don't worry. You can always borrow my favourite biker T-shirt. It's perfect. The back says, 'If you can read this, the girlfriend fell off'!'"

Poker game forgotten, the women enthusiastically joined in the hypothetical escapade.

Placing her cards face down, Pat said, "Well, if we are going to be Hooters on Scooters, then we have to embrace the whole theme of the night. We all have to wear a pair of leather chaps."

"With or without underwear?" Meg queried seriously, wearing her best poker face.

An immediate stunned silence fell over the room. Then the women dissolved into near hysteria, as each one grappled with the image that Meg's question brought up.

"Oh, please," Allie declared, pressing her hands to her eyes in mock horror. "Now it's just getting ugly."

"Oh my God," howled Daphne, gasping through her laughter. "Just imagine, how are we going to cope, trying to dodge all those flying insects that swarm around the headlights at that time of night?"

That suggestion prompted another round of hilarity which lasted several more minutes.

Finally regaining control, Sparrow managed to add, "Well, I for one will not be volunteering to work in the First Aid tent when you lot come in for your insect extractions."

"Well, the more demure amongst us could at least wear a G-string," Meg joked, winking at Sparrow.

Allie screwed up her face at the thought. "Ugghhh, who wants to have a little strip of material between their cheeks all night? I'd be squirming the whole time trying to get comfortable."

Pat rose from the table to demonstrate as she said, "I can just see us—walking around tugging on our G-strings."

"Besides," added Daphne, trying valiantly to keep a straight face. "I don't think they make them in my size."

"Well, Daph, one thing's for sure," Allie managed through her laughter, tears rolling down her cheeks. "You sure as hell can't wear your cottontails under your chaps. That would be like setting a spinnaker on your Vespa and sailing up Oxford Street. We wouldn't be able to keep up with you."

Pat slung her arm around Daphne's shoulders. "Oh, you should do it just for the hell of it."

Sparrow gasped. "You all have to stop. My ribs are hurting from laughing so much. You're going to give me a coronary".

Sanity eventually returned to the room and the women made a half-hearted attempt to renew their card game amidst sporadic giggling.

Pat chortled quietly over her newly dealt hand of cards. "Well, we may have a few years under our collective belts, but we sure as hell still can have a good laugh at ourselves. I can't remember the last time I had such fun, and I don't just mean the cards." She looked at her friends "Thanks for tonight. It was just what I needed. You are one crazy bunch of women."

"These days sixties and seventies are the new forties and fifties. Just because society thinks we're old, it doesn't mean we have to act like it," Daphne said.

Meg fixed her with a steely glare. "We are not old, Daphne," she said imperiously. "We are 'Women of a Certain

Age',' with a great deal of life still to live. 'Old' sounds like a description of my grandmother."

"Hideously proper and dignified, which doesn't sound like us at all," Allie insisted.

"I have to agree," Sparrow added. "When my grandmother was my age, although she kept fairly active, it was as if she had lived her life and was just waiting to die. The thought of travelling, or doing anything remotely adventurous, would have totally shocked her."

"So now that you have that information, Pat, you will have to go and tell Bella about our plans for the Mardi Gras," Allie said. "She'll probably think we've all finally gone mad."

"Oh, I'm not so sure." Pat grinned. "Knowing you all as well as she does, the only thing that would surprise her about this plan is that it took us so long to think of it!"

Chapter 12

DAPHNE ANXIOUSLY CHECKED THE CLOCK for the third time in fifteen minutes. She was due for dinner at Sparrow's home at seven p.m., and she couldn't believe time was moving so slowly.

She didn't know why she was so nervous; she and Sparrow had spent much of their time together over the past weeks. However, this was the first time either had invited the other for dinner, and Daphne suspected tonight was going to see their relationship move to the next level. *Well*, she thought with a smile, *I damned well hope it will.*

Daphne couldn't believe that at sixty-eight she was taking another shot at romance, especially after her utter determination to stay single. She knew this was what she wanted; she just had to get over her initial apprehension. Checking her reflection in the mirror, she grinned.

"Never say never, old girl," she chided herself.

Collecting her gifts from the kitchen, Daphne made her way to the front door. She had carefully chosen a bottle of red wine that came highly recommended by the local wine merchant and as a last minute thought, had also purchased a small bunch of flowers. It had been so many years since Daphne had dated anyone, but she assumed that wine and flowers still made a good impression. She locked the front door, and waved when she saw her neighbours walking arm in arm, out for their evening stroll. Daphne decided it was a perfect omen for the night ahead.

The western complex of the village, where Sparrow and Daphne lived, consisted of a dozen small cottages set amidst bush land. As Daphne made her way to Sparrow's, she admired the native gardens that surrounded the homes. The wattle trees were already in flower and within a few weeks, Daphne knew, the prolific banksia bushes would burst into a riot of red and yellow, brightening up the usual grey-green of the bush.

At Sparrow's front door, she took a deep breath before knocking firmly. Sparrow quickly opened the door, her face radiating joy and warmth. Suddenly, Daphne's nerves vanished.

"Hello," Sparrow said shyly, leaning up to receive Daphne's soft kiss on her cheek.

"Hi," Daphne breathed back, presenting the wine and flowers. "These are for you. I hope you like them."

Sparrow took the flowers and buried her face in them, inhaling deeply. "Oh, sweet peas." She smiled with delight. "They are my absolute favourites. Come into the kitchen with me while I find a vase for them."

Closing the door behind her, Daphne followed Sparrow into the kitchen. She had visited on a number of occasions over the past few weeks, and she enjoyed the warm and welcoming atmosphere of Sparrow's small, open-plan cottage. The furnishings, like Sparrow, were feminine without being fussy, creating a comfortable and homey feel.

Daphne hadn't given much thought to furnishing her own home. Her years in the Army had taught her to live simply. Occasionally she thought about getting more furniture, but she hadn't ever been bothered enough to get around to it. The first time she had invited Sparrow over, she'd suddenly seen the worn, mismatched furniture through different eyes and felt the need to apologise for her meagre surroundings. Sparrow had laughed away her attempted apology. "I don't care if you live in a shoe box," she'd said, taking Daphne's hand. "If that's what makes you happy, then that's fine. You don't need to impress me with fancy furnishings. I'm impressed already."

Sparrow handed Daphne the corkscrew, drawing her back from her reflections.

"Could you do the honours with the wine," she asked, indicating the bottle Daphne had brought with her, "while I arrange these flowers? We are having rack of lamb and roast vegetables, and then strawberries and homemade ice cream for dessert. Does that sound all right with you?"

Daphne closed her eyes. "That sounds wonderful." She groaned appreciatively. "And it smells even better."

"Well, I always think a roast is safe. It's hard to meet someone who doesn't like roast lamb." She placed the vase of sweet peas in the centre of the low table in front of the sofa.

Daphne paused, studying her host for a moment. Sparrow was looking particularly stunning in a pair of loose-fitting black pants, a black and gold silk blouse and soft black leather sandals. Small diamond earrings winked in the light and her grey hair looked so soft that Daphne longed to run her fingers through it.

"I just want to say how lovely you look this evening," she said softly.

"Thank you," Sparrow murmured, smiling as a faint blush spread over her cheeks. Taking the proffered glass of wine, she lightly touched Daphne's hand. "You're looking very handsome too."

Sparrow was unable to tear her eyes from Daphne's face until the soft chime of a timer in the kitchen broke the spell between them.

"Well, that brought us back to earth." Sparrow laughed as she reluctantly returned to her preparations for the meal.

They chatted easily together, discussing recent events, until Sparrow announced she was ready to serve dinner.

"Do you need any help?" Daphne rose from her stool at the kitchen bench and refilled both their wine glasses.

"Well, as a matter of fact, I was wondering if you wouldn't mind carving the lamb. I always seem to make rather a mess of it."

Daphne smiled. "I would be more than delighted."

As Sparrow picked up the wine glasses, Daphne took the platter containing the fragrant roast, and followed her into the small dining area. Placing it gently on the table, she stepped back, overwhelmed at the scene in front of her. The table had been set with one of Sparrow's beautifully hand-embroidered tablecloths, the threads adding splashes of colour against the soft butter cream of the linen. Small silver bowls of steaming vegetables had already been placed on the table, together with an ornate silver gravy boat and a crystal bowl containing mint jelly. The heavy cutlery at each setting shone, and the crystal glasses reflected the light of two candles that burnt softly at the centre of the table.

"Sparrow, this is just...beautiful," Daphne whispered.

Taking Sparrow's face in her hands, Daphne leant down and kissed her gently. Delighted by Sparrow's passionate response, Daphne leant in, pulling her closer as their kiss deepened, momentarily lost in Sparrow's soft lips. After a moment, her senses buzzing, Daphne gently broke the kiss.

"I want to kiss you until the sun comes up," she murmured softly, "but it would be a terrible waste not to eat this wonderful meal first."

Sparrow reached up, running her hands across Daphne's strong shoulders. "I hope you want to do more than just kiss me," she whispered back.

Groaning, Daphne ran her thumb over Sparrow's lips, already missing the feel of them against her own. "Oh, you have no idea, my darling."

Daphne smiled as she felt a shiver run through Sparrow at her words.

Sparrow took her hand and led Daphne to the table. "Well, I had better feed you so that you have plenty of energy."

Watching Daphne carve the lamb, Sparrow luxuriated in the joy that had been cautiously growing over the last weeks. For the first time in years, she had found someone she really cared for, someone she believed she could love. The fact that neither of them had been looking for someone added yet another layer of magic to the romance. When Daphne handed Sparrow her plate, their eyes met, and Daphne's smile caused Sparrow to catch her breath.

As Daphne sat, Sparrow raised her glass. "*Bon Appetit.*"

Daphne gently clinked her glass with Sparrow's, the sweet chime making them both smile.

"Have you seen anything more of Pat?" Sparrow asked, handing Daphne the gravy.

"As a matter of fact, she called in to see me this morning. Bella was having some friends over and shooed her out of the house. We had a great morning together sitting in my living room watching football replays. Then I made us a scratch lunch and we watched the match together and argued about referee decisions. I think she and Bella are starting to work their issues out. Pat certainly seems more relaxed, which is a relief. This morning it was just like old times."

"Is there any more news on how the chemo treatment is going?"

Daphne took a sip of wine. "No, but they are trying to stay optimistic. Bella was wearing a beanie when I was there last. Pat said she has lost nearly all her hair now."

Sparrow shook her head. "I can't imagine what they are going through. The first time would have been bad enough, but for them to be hit a second time, seems so damned unfair. I put myself on the roster with Allie to visit Bella next week. I don't really know either of them, but I'll do anything to help if I can."

Daphne agreed. "Well, the visits to Bella will certainly help. In the meantime, I'll look after Pat."

Helping herself to more vegetables, Sparrow looked over to Daphne. "I'm curious, how did the two of you become such good friends?"

Daphne chuckled. "When I first arrived here, I kept pretty much to myself. One day, there was a knock at my door. When I opened it, there was Pat with a six pack in her hand. 'I hear you are a West Tigers supporter,' she said. 'I have beer and no television at present. If you are watching the game, can I join you?' We have been the best of friends ever since. From that day on, Pat and Bella pretty much adopted me. There were times I was spending more time at their place than I was at mine."

The meal passed quickly as Daphne regaled Sparrow with stories of some of the antics she, Pat and several other residents had gotten up to over the last couple of years.

Daphne sighed as she swallowed her last mouthful.

"Sparrow, that was the best meal I have eaten in a long time."

Sparrow beamed. "Well, you have no idea how wonderful it is to have someone to cook for who appreciates food."

Daphne laughed. "I always appreciate food, but I must say, living by myself has made me lazy. I should eat better, but so many nights it's just too hard to get inspired. Heaven only knows what I would do without frozen meals."

"Well, I think you can forget about the frozen meals from now on, don't you?" Sparrow asked gently, standing to clear the plates. As Daphne rose to assist her, Sparrow motioned her to stay where she was. "No, sit there. I'll bring out the dessert."

———— ✦ ————

Daphne listened to Sparrow moving about in the kitchen, incredibly moved that she had gone to so much trouble to ensure that the evening was perfect. Over the last weeks, Daphne had felt herself falling in love with Sparrow a moment at a time. While thrilled at the wonder of it, she was still conscious of her fear of such an overwhelming change.

Realising she felt like a teenager on her first date, Daphne chuckled.

"What are you thinking about that is making you laugh?" Sparrow asked as she entered the room carrying dessert.

Colouring, Daphne gave a small cough. "Nothing, just…"

Sparrow placed a large bowl of plump strawberries and a salver of thick beaten cream between them, then handed Daphne a large spoon. Sparrow glanced across at her with a coy smile and raised eyebrow.

"Help yourself."

Over dessert, Daphne was quiet. It felt like a million butterflies had been let loose inside her and even the sweet strawberries were difficult to swallow. She glanced across at Sparrow, their eyes met and she felt her heart race. Putting her spoon down quickly before she dropped it, Daphne took a deep breath, surreptitiously wiping her sweating hands on her napkin.

"Can I help you wash up?" she asked as Sparrow rose.

Sparrow laid a hand on Daphne's shoulder as she leant in to collect her bowl. "No, I'm going to put it all in the dishwasher and press the button. Why don't you take a seat in the living room and make yourself comfortable? Would you like tea or coffee? I also have decaf, if you would prefer."

"Decaf would be perfect." Glad for the opportunity to be up and moving around, Daphne gave a small stretch and felt the tension ease out of her shoulders. She moved over to the living room, leaning forward to catch the gentle scent of the sweet peas as she took a seat on the sofa.

"If you enjoy cooking, you should get together with Allie and Bella," she remarked. "They often share recipes and experiment with food. As recipients of their efforts, Pat and I are always encouraging them."

"Allie has spoken to her about that," Sparrow replied. "Unfortunately, with the chemo, the last thing Bella wants to do is be around food. However, she has promised Allie that once she is well again the three of us will spend an afternoon together."

As the music flowed through the speakers, Daphne felt a sense of peace steal over her. Her previous nervousness had settled into a heightened sense of anticipation. Watching her prepare the coffee with such care, Daphne knew Sparrow shared her anticipation, and when she swore softly after spilling the sugar, Daphne suspected she also shared her nervousness.

Sparrow walked back into the living room, carrying a tray containing a coffee press, mugs, milk and sugar. Daphne moved the flowers to one side so she could set the tray down on the low table.

Taking a seat on the sofa next to Daphne, Sparrow poured a coffee. Their fingers brushed as she handed it over. For a long moment, neither of them moved, until Daphne deliberately took the coffee and placed it back on the tray. Taking Sparrow's face in her hands, she gently brushed their lips together.

Sparrow met Daphne's kiss eagerly. Daphne's lips ignited a response she had almost forgotten ever existed and a whimper escaped as she deepened the kiss. Daphne eased back to catch her breath, but Sparrow had other ideas. Leaning in closer, she pulled Daphne to her, as if absorbing every ounce of her. As Daphne responded and wrapped Sparrow in her arms, she thought she might explode, the press of Daphne's body against her own fuelling her desire.

Sparrow drew back, her chest heaving. She stood and took Daphne's hand, tugging her to her feet. Bringing her close, Sparrow looked up.

"While the last thing I want to do right now is stop, I do think the two of us would be much more comfortable in my bed."

Leading the speechless Daphne, Sparrow quickly moved to her bedroom. She paused near the bed, turned and slowly began unbuttoning Daphne's shirt. Sliding the shirt from her broad shoulders, Sparrow slowly reached around and released the clasp on Daphne's bra, freeing her small, soft breasts. She pressed her cheek to Daphne's breastbone, feeling the pounding of her heartbeat vibrating through her. Sighing deeply and wrapping her arms around Daphne's strong body, Sparrow savoured the sheer joy of an intimate contact she had never expected to feel again.

Gently, she turned her face, her lips softly tracking their way to Daphne's breasts. Taking a nipple in her mouth, Sparrow gently flicked her tongue over the nub.

"Sparrow..." Daphne moaned. She tried to free herself from Sparrow's mouth, but Sparrow held her tight.

"Shhhh, just let me," Sparrow whispered. "I have been dreaming of this since that night at the pool when you held me. Remember?"

"I've thought of little else since it happened. But you seem to have far too many clothes on," Daphne murmured, plucking at Sparrow's blouse.

Sparrow turned her face up and saw the arousal in Daphne's eyes. Acknowledging Daphne's point, she smiled.

"Well, then, I think we should undress each other, don't you?" she whispered.

Sparrow closed her eyes as she felt Daphne run her hands across the front of her body, quickly undoing the buttons and sliding her blouse from her shoulders. Their clothes rapidly dropped to the floor, until both were completely naked.

Sparrow looked at Daphne, hardly able to breathe. Her body offered a strength and softness that Sparrow longed to lose herself in. Drawing Daphne close, she let her hands and mouth sensuously discover gentle contours, finding the tender skin of her breasts, the womanly swell of her hips and belly, imprinting the feel and taste of the woman in her arms.

"God, you're beautiful," she breathed, tracing her fingers lightly over Daphne's breasts, kissing the trail of goosebumps left in their wake.

Taking Daphne's hand, Sparrow gently led her the last few short steps to the bed. She lifted back the covers and turned to her.

"Take me to bed, Daphne, and show me all those things you want to do to me."

—◆◇◆—

Daphne stood stock still, trying to comprehend the boldness of this tiny woman, not daring to move for fear of breaking the overwhelming feelings that were consuming her. Sparrow's earnest entreaty jolted her out of her fugue.

Daphne gently eased Sparrow onto the bed. Sparrow held her close, while Daphne tried to hold some of her weight off Sparrow. As a tremor ran through Daphne's arms, Sparrow spoke quietly.

"Daphne, I'm not going to break. We may not be in the first flush of youth and neither of us are up to Kama Sutra positions, but I need to feel you against me, all of you, and I need both of us to be comfortable. Just take your time and love me. Trust me, if it becomes uncomfortable, I'll let you know."

Daphne relaxed, planting whisper-soft kisses along Sparrow's jaw line. As their lips met in a searing kiss, Daphne slowly lowered her body fully onto Sparrow. Sighing in wonder, she felt Sparrow's legs wrap around her thighs, her wetness warm against Daphne's belly. Unable to maintain her control, she let her body take over.

"I need to touch you," Daphne panted, lifting herself up and positioning herself next to Sparrow. Daphne lowered her head to Sparrow's breasts, while her hands moved to the other woman's centre.

As her fingers explored Sparrow, she felt the urgency in her response and met Sparrow's surge with her own, the mixture of such strength, power and incredible tenderness bringing them both to shattering orgasm much sooner than either was prepared for.

<hr />

Cradled in each other's arms, the two women slowly recovered.

"If I had known you were going to cause that reaction in me, I would have suggested this much sooner," Sparrow whispered sometime later, running her hands over Daphne's body. "I know it's been a long time, but I think you've melted my bones."

Drawing her close, Daphne chuckled. "You know, there are people out there that would say we're too old for this."

Sparrow gently slapped her. "Don't you dare say that! Sex isn't just for the young, you know, no matter what they tell you." Sparrow kissed Daphne's breast. "We're never too old, we just take a little longer to recover. I may not be able to walk properly for the next week." She laughed.

Daphne looked at Sparrow in alarm. "I didn't hurt, you did I? I was trying so hard to be as gentle as possible. If I..."

Sparrow interrupted her with a kiss. "You would never hurt me," she said gently. "It's just that our bodies don't always cooperate like they used to."

"Oh, I don't know," Daphne murmured, nibbling Sparrow's shoulder. "I thought your body cooperated beautifully."

"Hmmm," Sparrow breathed softly in Daphne's ear. "I think we need to work more on yours. I am told you can never have enough practice."

"What an excellent idea," Daphne agreed as she felt Sparrow move down the bed. "They do say practice makes perfect..."

Chapter 13

LOUISE PARKED THE CAR IN what seemed to be the last available space for miles. Berry's bimonthly farmer's market was already in full swing and it was only nine-thirty in the morning. Louise had planned to spend the day working, but Caro had had other ideas.

"You can't just keep working," she'd remonstrated. "It's the weekend and we both need a break. We're going to the markets and that's that."

After locking the car, they followed the sizeable crowd to Berry Memorial Park. Boasting over 200 stalls, the market attracted people from all over the region. Caro and Louise tried to visit as often as possible; they loved the rich assortment of local produce for sale, as well as the opportunity to catch up with many of their friends.

Looking around at the crowd, Louise shook her head. "I think it's even busier than the last time we came," she said, neatly sidestepping a small child with a large stick of fairy floss.

"Well, it's been a while since we were last here. Probably three months at least," Caro replied.

The market was divided into three distinct sections. At the far end were the sheds that held the livestock. Farmers from all over the district came to buy and sell, and as a younger, more affluent group of farmers moved into the region, the livestock on offer had expanded from the usual cattle, pigs and sheep to include exotic breeds such as alpacas and llamas. A small shed displaying homemade craft works was dwarfed by the largest and most popular of the three, which housed the locally made foods and organic produce.

As they wandered, Louise soon realised that Caro was gently, but deliberately, steering them towards the large sheds where the animals were sold. Knowing her lover's inability to walk away from a homeless creature, she followed reluctantly.

"You do know that we aren't getting any more pets, don't you? And we are certainly not getting an alpaca," Louise declared, trying to deflect Caro's obvious enthusiasm.

Caro stopped and indicated the six large wire crates in front of her; each held half a dozen different breeds of hen

"So, I was thinking," Caro spoke quickly, before Louise could open her mouth again, "how sensible it would be to have some hens. I mean, just a couple of hens. Then we would have fresh eggs every day. There's plenty of space for them to roam during the day. We already have that old chook house we can fix up, and they will eat all sorts of food scraps. Just think, darling, fresh eggs whenever you want and as an added bonus, we get to recycle all our food scraps. They are not even expensive; I mean, if we got four they would pay for themselves in eggs in about four months. What we don't use ourselves, we can sell to the residents."

Louise glanced at Caro and then the hens. Despite herself, she could see the sense in Caro's suggestion, but after over fifteen years together, she knew better than to give in too quickly.

"At the beginning of the conversation it was two hens, and it is now four hens," she noted, her lips curving into a smile despite her best efforts to remain serious.

The owner of the hens wandered over to join them. "Well," he said with a grin, "there is no point just having two hens, and you have to have an even number otherwise they fight. Four is good, six is better."

"Good grief, it's a conspiracy." Louise laughed. "All right, then, I surrender. But four, not six; there are only so many eggs even we can eat."

After selecting the hens and arranging with the owner to deliver them after the market closed, they wandered over to the produce stalls, Louise's favourite part of the market. Their first stop was a stall run by renowned local cheese maker Amy Bowers.

"Hello, Amy, what cheeses have you brought today?" Louise asked, inspecting the mouth-watering array.

"Ah, just the people I needed to see," Amy replied. "I've been experimenting with a new soft cheese, and I think I might have finally perfected it. I'd love your opinion."

Amy cut two small slivers of the cheese and placed them on wafer biscuits, then handed the morsels over and stood waiting for their response.

Louise groaned as she savoured the offering. The piquant flavour was a wonderful contrast to the creamy softness of the cheese.

"Oh that's perfect," exclaimed Caro. "Just enough bite to catch your attention, but a wonderful creamy consistency."

Amy was delighted. "Well, judging by the reaction from you and the rest of my clients here today, it looks like it might turn out to be my signature cheese. I already have more orders than I can handle, but I have a secret supply for my most favourite customers if you want some."

Caro and Louise promptly ordered as much as Amy could spare, along with some of her other homemade delicacies.

"So how are things at OWL's?" Amy asked, packing up their olives, honey and cheeses.

"Flat out," Louise replied, taking the proffered packages. "The tenth anniversary party is really gathering a head of steam. All the invitations have been sent; the Wollongong, Sydney and Canberra Gay and Lesbian Choirs are booked; local and national media will be there."

"And you have to promise that you will enjoy yourself and not just stay in the kitchen doing the food preparation. We want to show off our wonderful local food merchants to all those rich party types from Sydney!" Caro admonished, then lowered her voice. "You never know, you might meet Ms Right. There will be lots of eligible women attending."

Amy smiled. "The invitations are gorgeous and I got mine yesterday. I've been busy working on new recipes for the day, which I hope you'll love." Sighing, she shook her head at Caro. "And yes, I promise to mingle afterwards, though I'm not holding my breath for Ms Right to walk into my life."

"Wait till they've tasted your food. I can guarantee you will get swamped with offers." Caro grinned. "I will personally introduce you to all the ones who won't break your heart."

Waving them off with a laugh, Amy turned to serve other customers. Caro and Louise continued to wander around, visiting with friends and filling their baskets. While paying for some homemade verjuice from the local winegrower, they ran into Meg and Allie. The four agreed that they were all shopped out, so Caro and Louise suggested coffee and cake at one of the local tea shops.

———— ✦❥✦ ————

"I think this must be one of the best markets I've been to," Meg commented, sitting down with a sigh of relief.

"Much less scary than that market at Marrakesh. You and your great ideas," Allie reminded her with a shudder.

At Caro and Louise's enquiring looks, Meg started to relate the story.

"We were in Morocco and all our friends told us we had to visit the Berber Market at Marrakesh. We were just wandering around when we realised we were being followed by a man. He must have seen that we had spotted him, because he approached Allie and asked her a question in Arabic."

"He was tall, dark and rather scary," Allie interjected. "He just kept asking me the same question. I had absolutely no idea what he was saying, but he was getting quite persistent. Then he pulled out this huge knife and brandished it about before suddenly grabbing a handful of my hair. I thought he was going to decapitate me."

"What on earth did he want?" Caro asked, fascinated, as their orders were delivered to the table.

Meg poured herself and Allie cups of coffee while she waited for the waitress to finish and everyone to settle. She smiled. "It turned out that he quite literally wanted Allie's hair. She had beautiful golden hair which was quite long at the time. I believe the story was that it was so unusual and rare that he would be able to trade it for ten camels or something."

"So what happened?" Louise asked, helping herself to a lemon tart.

"Well, luckily there was a local in the crowd who spoke English and he was able to explain that while we were very honoured, we would rather him not cut Allie's hair. Eventually, he got the message and left..."

"...and we caught a taxi straight back to the hotel," Allie finished. "We left Marrakesh the next day."

Meg looked affectionately at her friend and placed a reassuring hand on her arm. "You weren't in danger, you know. It was all under control."

"I agree with Allie. I'd have panicked if some swarthy male had been waving a large knife at me too," Caro sympathised.

"Exactly how long have you two known each other?" Louise asked, sipping her Earl Grey tea.

Allie smiled at Meg. "Over forty years. We met at a mutual friend's party. I was the protected daughter of a suburban doctor, and I thought Meg was the most glamorous and exotic woman I had seen in my whole life."

"I had just gotten back from travelling around Europe," Meg added, sharing her cake with Allie. "I struck up a conversation with this cute, golden haired young woman and something just clicked with us. We ended up sharing a house together while Allie finished her chef's apprenticeship."

Allie shook her head. "Oh my goodness, those were some pretty wild times. I can't remember the number of mornings we would stumble home from some party or other and I would have to jump in the shower and go straight to work. It's a wonder I was allowed to finish my apprenticeship."

Meg waved her hand dismissively. "Well, the fact that you were a far better chef than your instructor may have had something to do with it."

"Anyway, we have been the closest of friends ever since," Allie said.

Louise thought she saw a fleeting expression cross Meg's face at Allie's words, but she had no sooner noticed it than it vanished.

"So, how are the preparations for the anniversary party coming along?" Meg asked.

Louise smiled. "I've had the distinct pleasure of being able to tell several people who have rung me this week that the reason they don't have an invitation is because they weren't sent one."

Caro leant forward confidentially. "It took ten years, but boy, karma is sweet."

"Ahh, so that sound I hear is certain members of the cliterati gnashing their collective teeth?" Meg quipped.

"Oh, Meg, that is such a perfect image," Louise said through the laughter.

Caro looked at her watch, then over at Meg and Allie. "Well, we had better start heading back home. We have some hens being delivered and I want to make sure that their accommodation is up to scratch, excuse the pun, before they arrive."

Walking out into the afternoon sunshine, the four women said their goodbyes. Caro watched as Meg and Allie walked away, arms linked, bodies leaning into one another.

"Best friends, phooey," she remarked to Louise. "Did you see the expression on Meg's face when Allie announced they were the 'closest of friends'? If they're not lovers, then they damned well should be."

Laughing, Louise placed a soft kiss on the top of her head. "I've had a wonderful day. Thanks for prying me out of the office and insisting I come; it was just what I needed."

"We both needed the break, and the day, my darling, is not over yet. When we get home, I am going to put you in a hot bubble bath while I check the chicken house and get the new arrivals settled. Then we are turning off phones and computers and having a quiet, romantic picnic dinner."

Seeing the anticipation in her lover's eyes, Caro pulled her close.

Louise nestled in. "And after dinner?" she whispered seductively.

Caro took Louise's hand and kissed her palm. "There will be a very special, personalised dessert."

Chapter 14

ALLIE STOOD AND STRETCHED, DELIGHTED to hear her back crack as she gently twisted her torso. She had been engrossed in a particularly good book and was surprised to find that it was already after midnight. As she reached over to close her curtains, her attention was caught by a blue flashing light across the road. Curious, she went to her front door and was confronted by the sight of several cars and an ambulance. It took a moment for her to register that they were parked outside of Meg's cottage. Without thinking, Allie raced across the road, reaching the door just as they were lifting Meg onto a gurney.

"Meg," Allie shouted, running over to where her friend lay. Looking down, she was horrified to see Meg pale and unconscious, her face covered by an oxygen mask.

"What is it? What's happened to her?" she demanded.

"Allie, it's all right." Jenny Wilcox, the on-call doctor, took hold of her arms. "The medical crew have got her and they are taking her to the hospital."

"But why? What's happened?" As she spoke, the medical team began moving Meg out the door and to the ambulance. Allie tried to follow. "Where are they taking her? I...I need to go with her. I don't want her to be alone."

Jenny put her arm around Allie's shoulder and drew her back inside. "Allie, I know you are distressed, but the medical staff are doing all they can. Believe me, she won't be alone."

Allie threw Jenny's arm off her shoulders and ran out to the ambulance. All she could see was Meg's face, pale and unresponsive.

"Damn it, I knew there was something wrong with her. She kept denying it and telling me it was nothing. She even got angry with me when I pushed her for an answer..." She turned back to Jenny, desperate. "What is it? What's happening?"

"We think it's a heart attack. Luckily she was able to get to the panic button on the wall of the cottage, but she was unconscious when we arrived." Jenny acknowledged the paramedics as they closed the ambulance doors, then turned back to Allie. "Listen, we urgently need Meg's medical power of attorney and the next of kin paperwork. Do you know where we could find it?"

Allie watched the ambulance pull away, blue lights flashing. "Yes, I have copies of both."

"Excellent. If you can grab them now, I can take you with me to the hospital."

Glad to have something concrete to focus on, Allie rushed over to her unit. She and Meg had arranged the paperwork when they'd first arrived at OWL's Haven. She grabbed the necessary documents from her desk drawer, then collected her phone, wallet and keys and hurried back outside. As she locked her door, Pat raced up.

"I've just heard. Is there anything we can do?"

Allie shook her head, aware of the panic threatening to overwhelm her.

"I'm going to the hospital with Dr Wilcox. I have no idea how long I'll be or..." Allie trailed off as tears filled her eyes.

Pat gave her a quick hug. "You can't go alone. I'll come with you."

Allie shook her head. "No, really, I just need to go."

Pat looked concerned. "Let us know what's happening. If you need anything, just call."

She gave Pat a quick hug, then hurried back to Jenny's car; the motor was still running and as Allie got in, they pulled away.

Caro and Louise rushed to the hospital when they heard what happened and learnt that Allie was there by herself. When she saw them walk into the waiting room, Allie rose, relieved, and gave them each a hug.

Louise looked at Allie carefully, concerned by how exhausted she looked. "What's happened? All we know is that Meg's had a heart attack."

After Allie confirmed that was all she knew, Louise took her hand and said gently, "Meg's in the best possible place. They will have her in ICU and will be monitoring her for everything. I know this feels really hard, but there's not much we can do but sit and wait until they have something to tell us. Jenny won't leave you waiting long."

Half an hour later, Caro brought in cups of takeaway coffee, water and muffins that she had managed to find for them all.

Louise took a sip and couldn't help but grimace when she tasted the coffee.

"Sorry, love," said Caro quietly. "It was all I could find. The cafeteria is closed, so vending machine coffee is as good as it gets. At least it will be marginally better than the tea."

Louise took Caro's hand. "It's OK, sweetheart. At least it gives us something to do." She scanned the nursing post yet again. "I just wish we could get some news."

Caro unwrapped the muffin and broke a piece off to hand to her lover. "I know, honey."

Looking over at Allie, whose coffee sat untouched in front of her, Louise frowned. After their initial conversation, Allie had barely said two words. She sat in a chair, her tension almost palpable, staring fixedly at the ICU doors as if willing someone to come through and give them some news.

"They can't be too much longer," Louise said. "They know we're here and Jenny won't keep Allie waiting unnecessarily."

At that moment, the swing doors opened and Jenny walked towards them. Acknowledging Caro and Louise with a nod, she went straight to Allie, giving a tired smile.

"It was touch and go there for a while, but it looks like Meg is going to pull through. Luckily, getting to her as quickly as we did meant that we were able to minimise any permanent damage."

Allie closed her eyes and slumped back in her chair, her immense relief evident on her face. "Was it a heart attack?" she asked hoarsely.

"Yes, and quite a severe one. She was incredibly lucky. Despite her heart, she is very fit for someone her age and that worked for her. She's probably going to need surgery, but for now she's stable. We will keep her in ICU for a few days and monitor her progress. Once we run some more tests we'll have a better idea of what to do next. The cardiologist will evaluate her more fully tomorrow."

Allie stood, and Louise and Caro joined her. "Can I see her, just for a moment? I really need to know she's OK."

The doctor nodded. "OK, but just for a few minutes." Jenny lightly touched her shoulder. "She's still unconscious, so don't be alarmed by all the equipment; it's just to let us know what's happening."

Allie turned to Caro and Louise.

"Go see her. We'll wait here until you're finished," Louise said softly.

Allie walked slowly into ICU and stood outside the curtained cubicle. Taking a deep breath, she gently pulled the curtain aside.

"Oh, Meg."

Despite having mentally prepared herself, Allie found herself gripping the bed rail. Meg lay unmoving, attached to a myriad of tubes and machines that beeped and whirred with every breath she took. Fighting back tears, Allie moved to Meg's side and gently clasped her hand.

"Meg Sullivan, I don't know if you can hear me, but there is something I need to say." Allie swallowed hard. "You are not going to die. You are going to get through this and wake up." Running her fingers through Meg's hair, Allie let the tears flow. "Please, Meg, please," she whispered.

Allie continued to talk to Meg quietly, hoping she could hear, hoping she might stir.

"It's good to do that."

Turning, she noticed a nurse standing by the foot of the bed.

"I always believe they can hear you. I think it helps to keep them connected."

Allie gave a wan smile. "It's about all I can do. I feel so damned helpless."

The nurse smiled kindly. "Well, if you want my professional opinion, what will probably really help is for you to go home and get some sleep. You look completely done in. She's got me, another nurse and all this equipment looking after her. You know we'll call you the minute anything changes."

Looking down at Meg, Allie nodded. "Thank you for letting me see her." Giving Meg a gentle kiss on the forehead, Allie turned to the nurse. "If she wakes up, will you tell her I'll be here in five minutes?"

Laughing, the nurse slowly walked Allie out of the ICU. "I'll write it on her chart to make sure. Now, let your friends take you home. I dare say I'll be seeing you tomorrow."

Back in the waiting room, Allie joined Caro and Louise.

"Are you OK?" Caro asked.

Allie nodded, exhaustion overtaking her.

Louise took her arm. "Come on then, let's get you home."

Chapter 15

SPARROW WOKE SLOWLY, ALLOWING HER other senses to take in her surroundings before she opened her eyes. The chorus of birds outside told her that it was a little later than she normally awoke. She was aware of the faint smell of fresh coffee and wondered if Daphne was up and making breakfast. Eager to find out, Sparrow threw on a light robe and hurried to the kitchen. A sliver of disappointment ran through her on finding the cottage empty, but a note propped up against the coffee pot caught her eye.

Honey,

I didn't want to wake you. I've gone to see if there is any news regarding Meg. I should be home about nine, but if I am going to be later, I'll ring you.

Daphne xx

Sparrow poured herself a cup of coffee and placed it in the microwave to reheat. It had been after midnight when Pat had arrived at Sparrow's door with the news of Meg's heart attack. Daphne had immediately dressed and gone with Pat to see if there was anything they could do to help. Returning within the hour with very little news, Sparrow knew that she was genuinely concerned about both Meg and Allie.

As she reread the note, Sparrow sincerely hoped that Meg would pull through. Their friendship was still relatively new, but Sparrow liked what she knew of the feisty woman a great deal. She also wondered about the relationship between Allie and Meg. Daphne said they were just friends, but Sparrow saw something else, something deeper, and wondered if either woman was aware of the undercurrent.

Hearing a key in the lock, Sparrow turned. Seeing Daphne walk through her front door still gave Sparrow a thrill and made her feel inexplicably shy.

"Good morning, my darling." Daphne gently lifted her face and kissed her on the lips.

Hearing the tenderness in Daphne's voice, Sparrow instinctively leant in to return the kiss, deepening it a fraction. She felt Daphne's arms go around her and leant further into her lover's arms, absorbing her warmth and strength.

Finally, Daphne surfaced, breathing heavily. Sparrow smiled mischievously, delighted at her reaction, and stepped away.

"Coffee?" she asked innocently, holding up a mug and grinning at the woman who now firmly held her heart.

Daphne took a deep breath. "Just what I need, more stimulation," she said ruefully, shaking her head.

Sparrow gave her a brief hug. "So, what did you find out about Meg?" she asked.

"We'll know more when Allie has had a chance to talk to the hospital and Dr Wilcox later today. She knew very little when I saw her before she left this morning. I guess we just have to wait and see."

Sparrow shook her head. "All that uncertainty doesn't make it easy, does it?" Finishing the last of her coffee, she placed the mug in the sink. "Well, hopefully the doctor will have good news. Poor Allie, she must be exhausted. Is there anything she needs?"

Putting her arms around Sparrow again, Daphne sighed. "Allie has asked me to let people know what's happening regarding Meg so I thought I'd pick up Pat and we could make a couple of house calls. I'm not even sure who knows Meg's in hospital. Do you mind if we postpone our plans until later?" she asked tentatively.

"Of course not. It's really important that you let people know," Sparrow agreed. "Keep me in the loop, won't you? If there is anything I can do…"

Daphne bent and brushed her lips against Sparrow's.

"Of course I will. Why don't I give you a ring in a few hours when I have a better idea of what the situation is?"

"OK, in the meantime I will make you something special for dinner." Sparrow offered with a smile.

"Or we could skip straight to dessert if you didn't feel like cooking," Daphne grinned cheekily.

"You are one bad woman," murmured Sparrow, "and I am so very lucky."

———————

Pat was making Bella a light breakfast when there was a knock at the door. She hurried down the hall and opened it, greeting Daphne with an anxious look.

"Have you heard anything new?"

Shaking her head, Daphne followed Pat back to the kitchen where the delicious smell of frying bacon reminded her that she had missed breakfast. Looking longingly at the bacon, she told Pat the only thing she knew, that Meg had suffered a heart attack.

"Damn, at least she is still fighting. How's Allie holding up?" Pat asked, handing her a coffee.

Just as Daphne was about to answer, Bella came into the kitchen, keen to hear the news. Daphne repeated what she knew for Bella's benefit. While they listened, Pat went to the fridge and pulled out more bacon and another two eggs as Bella reset the coffee pot.

"So what do we do now?" Pat asked as she put on more toast.

"Well, Allie's asked if we could just let some of their friends know what's happening. I imagine the jungle drums have already carried the story to most people, but because it all happened so late last night, there may be some that don't know. At least if we tell people it will keep them off Allie's back," she added, leaning against the kitchen bench.

"Funny, isn't it?" mused Bella, setting another place at the table for Daphne. "It's as if those two are a couple. I swear, I have never understood why they don't just admit they love each other and get on with it."

Pat raised an eyebrow at Daphne. "My ever practical spouse."

"Well, you know, Bella's right. I have to admit that I've often wondered about their friendship and Sparrow is positive that there is something going on under the surface."

Pat and Bella exchanged a smile. "So, how is Sparrow?" Bella asked casually, handing Pat a plate of toast. "We haven't seen much of her over the last couple of days."

"She's wonderful," Daphne replied happily, unable to stop the smile that spread across her face.

"So it's all going well then?" asked Pat.

"I can't believe how well it's going. I have to keep pinching myself."

Motioning Daphne to the table, Pat placed plates of eggs and bacon in front of her and Bella. "It's about time you found someone to share your life with."

Daphne looked at her two friends, then drew in a deep breath, her happiness receding. "To be honest, I am trying so hard not to let my fear take over. I really didn't want another relationship; there was so much pain from the last one. But somehow Sparrow just marched through every barrier I had without me even realising."

Pat refilled Daphne's mug and then took a seat at the table next to Bella.

"I've told Sparrow things about my life that almost no-one else knows." Shaking her head, Daphne picked up her cutlery. "Sometimes it feels too good to be true; I worry that someone or something is going to come along and rip it all away."

"Well, the only one that can do that is you," Bella said gently. "You need to trust yourself and trust Sparrow as well."

"I'm not very good at trusting, Bella. I seem to lurch from being ecstatically happy to being almost frozen in fear. I had forgotten how exhausting a new relationship can be."

Bella glanced at Pat. "Yes, it can be," she agreed, "but when you find the right person, nothing else matters."

Daphne smiled at them both and attacked her food with enthusiasm. Before Bella's illness, they had breakfasted regularly together, and the three slipped easily into their old routine. As they finished eating, Pat rose to take the empty plates to the sink.

"Leave those, darling," Bella said. "I'll put them into the dishwasher later. Why don't you and Daphne go and give everyone the news."

Pat seemed as if she was about to disagree, but after a moment's thought, went over and kissed Bella gently.

"Thank you, *cara*," Bella whispered quietly, stroking Pat's face.

When they parted, Daphne gave Bella a hug. "It was wonderful to share breakfast with you again. Just like old times."

"Well, I hope you won't leave it so long next time," Bella said, returning the hug. "You know you are always welcome and we would love for you to bring Sparrow as well."

Outside, Daphne and Pat headed off to their first duty call. As they walked, Daphne glanced over at her friend. "Is it my imagination, or is Bella looking better?"

Pat smiled. "No, it's not your imagination; we are both feeling so much more positive. Now that she's adjusting to the chemo, her appetite has increased, she's feeling stronger and her nausea is completely under control. I'm trying so hard not to get ahead of myself, but for the first time in almost a year, I am beginning to feel like we might be getting on top of it all. We still have a couple of months of chemo, but for now, we are both just enjoying her feeling almost normal."

Daphne slung an arm around Pat's shoulders. "That's fantastic news, my friend. I can't tell you how happy I am for you both. I know you were having an awful time of it there for a while."

"Well, I had to learn to let go...of everything. You know we have both been seeing a counsellor?"

Daphne nodded without comment.

"Yeah, well, as much as I dreaded the thought, once I started, I found it to be the best thing I could have done. I had no idea how much...stuff I had locked away in my head. Finding someone to talk to, who understood the situation, lifted a huge weight off me that I hadn't even realised was there. I began to understand that I was suffocating Bella with kindness and building up huge resentment in the process. Once I saw that, I was able to step back a little. It's still difficult at times, but I'm getting much better."

"You mean, like wanting to stay and wash the dishes this morning?" Daphne asked.

Pat shook her head and smiled. "You don't miss a trick, do you? But here I am, out with you, making house calls and not driving Bella mad by wrapping her up in cotton wool."

———— ✦❈✦ ————

Most of the people they spoke to about Meg asked when they could visit, leaving both women touched at the level of caring. After more than two hours, the pair were exhausted. As they neared her cottage, Pat turned to Daphne.

"Want to call in and have coffee? Bella's out and I've got the Tigers game from last night if you want to watch it with me."

Daphne hesitated, looking at her watch. "Thanks for the offer, but I should get back to Sparrow's. I promised her we'd spend some time together this afternoon."

Pat grinned, "Uh huh...you do that a lot in a new relationship." Dodging the playful slap she knew was coming, Pat turned towards her front gate. "If you hear anything from Allie later this afternoon, let me know. Thanks for the company."

Waving, Daphne laughed. "You too. Call you later."

Chapter 16

ALLIE LET HERSELF INTO MEG'S cottage, exhausted but reluctant to go back to her own place, choosing instead to surround herself with the familiarity of Meg's. She couldn't quite believe that less than twenty-four hours had passed since the heart attack. Pat and Bella had rung and invited her to stay with them, but after spending most of the day at the hospital, she just wanted to be alone, to not have to talk to anyone. That morning she and Dr Wilcox had discussed what Allie now understood were very likely symptoms leading up to Meg's attack. Jenny had promised to let Allie know as soon as she had spoken to the specialist.

Walking into the living room, she was relieved to see that it had been tidied and the assorted medical detritus disposed of. Placing her bag on the sofa, Allie went into the kitchen. As usual, everything shone—it was the one room in the house that was always tidy. Meg quite simply refused to cook, and Allie had long since given up trying to encourage her.

Allie prepared a cup of tea, worried, despite Dr Wilcox's assurances, that Meg was still unconscious. It had been nearly twenty-four hours; surely she would wake up soon.

"Stop it," Allie admonished herself out loud, pushing the tendrils of panic away. "Meg's going to be fine."

Gathering her tea, she made her way through the cottage, turning off lights and closing blinds. In Meg's room, she stopped suddenly. Meg's scent overwhelmed her, causing her to almost drop the cup from her trembling hands. Placing it carefully on Meg's dressing table, she entered the room slowly. The scarf Meg had bought at the markets was draped over the bedroom chair, a splash of vibrant gold and orange. Shoes, bags, newspapers and various clothing items were scattered around the room. Allie sat on the bed, running her hands over the luxurious coverlet before getting back up to fetch her tea.

Allie took it back to the bed, wrapping her hands around the delicate porcelain for warmth. Her eyes wandered around the room until they settled on a framed photo of herself and Meg. Putting her cup down, she stretched across the bed to pick it up from the side table. Smiling, she remembered the day the photograph had been taken. They'd been invited by friends to spend New Year's Eve in Banff, and had spent the day skiing a particularly tricky pass. Flushed with their success, they had treated themselves to a hot chocolate by the fire in the hotel. A roving photographer, selling photographs to visitors at the resort, offered to take their picture.

Running her thumb along the image of Meg's laughing face, Allie was engulfed by distress so thick she could almost taste it. Suddenly the prospect of losing Meg hit her, taking her breath away. Curling up in a ball on Meg's bed, Allie held the photo close to her chest and let the tears take over.

Chapter 17

"ALLIE."

She turned to see Dr Wilcox getting out of her car opposite Meg's cottage. Surprised, Allie fumbled with her car keys.

"Hello, Jenny. I was just going to the hospital to see Meg. I was there briefly last night when she regained consciousness, but she fell back asleep almost immediately. The nurses told me she'd probably be more alert today. I am so relieved she's okay."

Jenny looked hesitant. "I was planning on catching up with you at the hospital, but had to see a patient here, so I thought I'd call by on the off chance you were still here."

Allie looked steadily at the woman in front of her. "Should we talk inside?" she asked slowly, concern edging her voice.

Jenny nodded. "Do you mind? I need to bring you up to date with Meg's condition."

Allie turned and relocked her vehicle then walked across to Meg's cottage and opened the door, inviting Jenny through to the living room.

Refusing the offer of tea or coffee, Jenny sat on the sofa and clasped her hands in front of her. She looked at Allie, standing against the mantle. "Firstly, I'm really glad that Meg has come round. Two days is a long time to be unconscious and we were becoming concerned. However, the staff have spoken to her and she is coherent and responding well, and we are confident there are no neurological side effects."

Allie waited, arms crossed, for the rest.

"The full results of the tests have come through and the specialist has advised that we need to urgently operate. Meg has a serious problem with a heart valve and we're going to have to replace it. Normally, we would have tried to fix it with a relatively minor procedure, but it has gone too far and we have no choice but to do a much more invasive operation. The specialist is seeing Meg this morning and advising her, but I wanted to let you know personally."

Allie walked over to the sofa and sat next to Jenny. "So, how risky is this operation?"

"No operation is without risk, but Meg is in good condition for her age and that's a huge plus. The other great news is that we have a wonderful cardiac surgeon who specialises in this operation, so she is in the best hands."

Allie had a million questions. "So, when would she have it? Does she need to go to Sydney?"

"Well, as far as time frame, the sooner the better. The surgeon is looking at the next couple of days and because we have him here we don't need to transfer her to Sydney. He'll bring another doctor with him and our local staff are more than capable of assisting him."

"OK, well, that sounds positive." Allie paused and looked at Jenny, frowning. "You said something about fixing it with a simple operation. Why can't you do that?"

Jenny took a deep breath, choosing her words with care. "Remember when we talked a few days ago about whether Meg had been displaying symptoms in the lead-up to the attack?"

Allie nodded.

"Well, the surgeon believes that if she had come to us six to eight months ago when the symptoms first began, we could have identified the problem and likely been able to fix it with a minor operation."

Allie felt the shock of Jenny's words hit her, leaving her stunned. Shaking her head, she gazed incredulously at the doctor.

"Wait, so, so, what you're saying," she stuttered, as the import began to sink in, "is that if Meg had admitted to the symptoms at the beginning, it could have been fixed and she wouldn't have had the heart attack or needed this operation?"

Jenny hesitated. "Well, nothing is absolute in medicine, Allie…"

"But it's a distinct possibility, isn't it?" Allie said shortly.

Jenny nodded reluctantly. "Yes, I have to say, it would have made a huge difference."

Allie stood suddenly and walked back over to the mantle, her fists tightly clenched. Concerned, Jenny rose and joined her.

"Allie," she said softly. "I can't make any guarantees, but if it was someone I loved, I would want the team we have doing the operation."

Taking a deep breath, Allie turned to face her. "Thank you. I'm sure Meg will be in wonderful hands."

Jenny watched Allie struggling to maintain her composure. "Do you have any more questions? Is there anything else I can tell you?"

Allie shook her head briefly. "No, I'm fine. It's all very clear."

Jenny picked up her bag to leave. "Let me know when you get to the hospital. I know the specialist will have already spoken to Meg by now, but I am more than happy to talk to the two of you together and answer any questions."

Allie walked Jenny to the door. Opening it, she turned to face her with a polite smile. "Thank you for coming to let me know."

Jenny frowned, unsettled by Allie's sudden change in demeanour. "It's a lot to absorb, but the good news is, we've got a great team, and Meg's a fighter."

Watching Jenny wave as she drove away, Allie felt her anger simmering just below the surface.

"Damn you, Meg Sullivan," she said through gritted teeth, slamming the door. "Damn you for lying to me."

Allie stood with her forehead pressed against the closed door, trying to steady her breathing, working hard to subdue her anger. After a few moments, she took a deep breath and began to gather the few belongings she had brought over.

The anger she felt at Meg's behaviour, her ongoing denials that anything was wrong, affected her more deeply than she could have imagined. Through the numbness, she could feel a deep, swirling fury resonating through her body, looking for an escape. She knew she wouldn't be able to hold it in much longer and she urgently needed to get out of Meg's home. As she picked up her things from the bed, she inadvertently knocked the photo of the two of them to the floor; the glass smashed. Looking down in horror at the shattered photograph, Allie choked back a sob and fled back to her own cottage.

Chapter 18

"Ms Sullivan, can you hear me? Wake up now...Ms Sullivan," the nurse called, leaning over her patient.

Meg groaned, eyes slowly fluttering open. As panic began to seep into her consciousness, she felt the reassuring touch of warm fingers on her arm.

"It's all right, you're in post op and you've come through the surgery very well. We're just going to take you up to ICU."

Through a foggy haze, Meg felt like a lead weight was pressing on her chest. Somewhere in the distance, she registered there was pain. She tried to speak, but something in her throat prevented her from making any sound. As terror threatened to overwhelm her again, she brought her free hand up to her face, reaching for the breathing tubes.

The nurse gently took her hand and held it in place on the bed. "It's all right," she said reassuringly. "It's just a tube to help you breathe. Don't try and talk just yet."

Giving up the battle, Meg lapsed back into sleep.

When she next opened her eyes, Meg was aware of Jenny Wilcox smiling at her from the side of her bed.

"Well, it is nice to see you back in the land of the living, Meg."

Meg tried to speak, but Jenny laid a hand on her arm and shook her head.

"Don't try and speak just yet. I just need to check you, and the nurses need to finish getting you settled. Do you understand what I am saying?"

Meg nodded weakly.

"OK, I just need to check the stitches in your chest. It may feel a little uncomfortable, but I will be as quick and gentle as possible."

Meg nodded, trying hard to stay awake.

"Just try and hang on for a bit longer, Meg. I need to make sure that everything is okay."

Meg felt cool air as her chest was examined.

Apparently satisfied with her assessment, Jenny removed her gloves and spoke calmly, "Meg, the nurse is going to take your temperature and blood pressure and then we're done."

Within a few moments, the preliminaries were finished. The nurse spooned several ice chips from a cup on the bedside table into Meg's mouth. "Suck these slowly. It will help with the raspiness you are feeling."

Clearing her throat cautiously, Meg looked expectantly at the doctor.

"So, how did it go?" she croaked out in a whisper.

Jenny finished writing on Meg's chart, then sat on the chair next to the bed.

"Well, the surgeon is going to come see you tomorrow, but I can tell you that he was very pleased. It was a long operation, but it went like clockwork."

Meg closed her eyes, her thoughts going to Allie; she still didn't understand why her best friend had not been to see her before the operation.

"Can I have visitors?" she rasped.

"While you are here in ICU, maybe one at a time, but for no more than five minutes each. You've been through a major trauma and you're going to need a great deal of recovery time." Seeing Meg's eyes start to close, Jenny patted her hand. "For now, though, just sleep and regain your strength."

Meg had so many questions she wanted to ask, but she couldn't seem to stay awake. Maybe if she just closed her eyes, things would start to make sense...

Chapter 19

LOUISE UNLOCKED HER OFFICE WHILE digging her mobile phone out of her bag. Seeing Caro's number, she smiled.

"Hey, sweetheart, how's the Big Smoke?"

Caro was in Sydney for three days as a guest speaker at an international conference. "Busy, smoggy and humid, but apart from that, glorious."

Louise laughed. While she would always choose the country, she knew her partner still occasionally hankered for the fast city life. "Well, kick up your heels and enjoy it. You don't get there very often."

"Probably just as well. Have you any idea how expensive this damned city is? I'd need three jobs just to keep me in shoes."

Louise nodded. "Listen, darling, I rang you earlier to let you know that I've heard Meg has come out of the operation and she's responding well; very sore of course, but apparently the doctors are really pleased."

"Thank goodness." Caro sighed audibly. "I've been wondering how it went. I was going to ring you, but assumed you'd let me know when you heard something."

"I thought I'd see if Allie is home and get some more information from her," Louise replied, sitting back in her chair and putting her feet up on the desk.

"Now the operation is done and Meg's recovering, I'm sure she'll be keen to visit."

Louise gazed thoughtfully out of her office window. "Mmm, I hope so. It was odd that she refused to see Meg before the operation."

"Well, go see her and I'm sure she'll be fine. It was a pretty scary scenario for her; she probably felt more in control by staying away. Listen, I have to get back to the conference. I'll talk to you tonight."

After hanging up, Louise sat motionless at her desk for several minutes, thinking about her conversation with Caro. She felt there was something more going on with Allie and it worried her. Keen to put her mind at rest, she decided to walk over and have a quick chat. If it was as Caro said, she would probably be at the hospital anyway.

Louise was surprised when Allie answered the door.

"Louise." Allie smiled in welcome. "What a lovely surprise. Come in. I've just made a batch of biscuits."

Louise entered the cottage and was immediately assailed by the wonderful smell of baking. "Oh, Allie, and this is the week I was planning to start my diet," she said with a laugh.

"Phooey." Allie waved away the excuse. "You have to at least help, otherwise I'll end up eating them all and they'll be lifting me out of here with a crane."

Louise settled herself at the kitchen bench while Allie prepared the tea, and the two discussed favourite recipes. When she handed Louise her cup, Allie suggested sitting under the pergola. "I've been inside all day; I desperately need to be outside for a while."

As they made themselves comfortable outside, Allie asked with a smile, "So, what brings you for a visit?"

Louise took a sip of the fragrant tea. "Well, I heard that Meg was out of her operation and, although still in ICU, doing well. I was wondering if you had any more news?"

Allie slowly placed her cup on the table and looked across at Louise. "No," she said coldly.

Louise's shock must have registered on her face. "I…I just thought…" she stammered.

A flash of irritation crossed Allie's face. "I haven't seen Meg or been in contact with her since before the operation. I'm sorry, Louise, but it's personal and none of anyone's business. It's wonderful to see you, and I'm more than happy to talk to you about anything else, but I will not discuss Meg."

Louise's biscuit stuck in her throat and she quickly took a swallow of tea. Giving a gentle cough, she tried desperately to think of something to say.

Allie softened her tone. "Louise, it's…OK. I know you are trying to help, but please, don't. What's done is done." Allie shrugged.

Louise looked at her. "Are you alright? Do you need anything?"

Allie gave a tight smile and shook her head. "Just to not talk about this, please."

Flustered and embarrassed, Louise nodded. "Of course, sorry…"

When she finished her tea, unable to cope with the undercurrent of tension any longer, Louise rose. "I'd better get back to the office. Caro's away and I have a mountain of paperwork." Seeing Allie rise, Louise motioned her back into her chair. "No, stay here in the sun. I can let myself out. Thanks for the tea. I'll…see you soon."

Once back out front, Louise blew out a huge breath. "What the hell was that about?" she asked herself quietly.

In the hope of getting to the truth, she walked slowly to Pat and Bella's.

Pat greeted her at the door. "Louise, come in."

"I just wanted to call in and say hello. I hope I'm not interrupting anything," Louise said as she followed Pat into the sunny living room.

"Louise." Bella rose from the sofa to give her a hug. "How wonderful to see you."

Louise looked affectionately at the two women. "Well, you're both certainly looking better than the last time I saw you," she said with delight.

"Sit, sit," Bella said. "Can we make you a cup of tea?"

Louise shook her head. "No, I just had one with Allie… in fact, that's sort of why I'm here."

Pat sat on the arm of Bella's chair.

Louise frowned. "I heard that Meg got out of surgery this morning, and I walked over to see if Allie had any more information. When I arrived she was fine, chatting and laughing, but the minute I asked about Meg, there was this shutter that slammed down, completely blocking everything. She not only resolutely refused to discuss her, but was obviously angry when I asked. I know it's really none of my business, but I'm concerned. Do you two know what's going on?"

Pat and Bella exchanged looks.

Seeing their awkwardness, Louise leant forward. "No, I'm sorry, I shouldn't have asked. It's personal and I don't want to put you in a difficult situation."

Pat rubbed her hand over her short hair. "To tell you the truth, Louise, we are as concerned as you are. Apparently, Allie discovered that Meg's operation was very likely avoidable."

Louise frowned. "I don't understand. She had a serious problem with one of her heart valves."

Pat nodded. "Yes, but what you probably don't know, and what Allie didn't know until just before Meg's op, was that if she had told someone about her symptoms when they first started happening, it's very possible it would have been able to be fixed with fairly minor surgery. Instead, Meg kept denying the symptoms until her heart finally gave up."

Louise sat back as the pieces began falling into place. "And Allie's angry that Meg didn't tell her," she said slowly.

"Furious and deeply hurt," Bella replied. "Allie had begun to notice something was wrong almost four months ago and despite repeated questioning, Meg kept denying it and brushing her off."

Louise frowned. "But why? Why would Meg risk her life like that?"

"Meg has a hatred of illness. She grew up with a mother who made illness an occupation. She sees it as a weakness, not always in others, but certainly in herself." Pat shrugged. "It's likely she didn't realise the seriousness of the symptoms. It's not the first time she's done this and it's driven Allie crazy in the past, but this may actually be the final straw. She arrived on our doorstep after the conversation with Jenny. We've never seen her so distressed and angry."

"Well, she was pretty upset when I brought the subject up. I didn't know what to say."

Bella nodded. "She needs to work this through, but it's going to take some time." Glancing up at Pat, Bella frowned. "The other problem is going to be trying to explain it all to Meg. At this stage she's only allowed one or two visitors a day, but once they take her out of ICU, she's really going to start wondering where Allie is. Pat and I will tell her, but not yet. She's got enough on her plate and we don't want her to have any setbacks."

Louise agreed. Rising to her feet, she said, "Well, ladies, I should leave you to your afternoon and get back to work. Thanks for filling me in, and I will keep it confidential. I plan to call in to see Meg later in the week."

"We're scheduled for tomorrow, fifteen minutes only, but it will be great to see her and confirm she is on the mend. When she asked them about the recovery period, the doctors did warn her that one of the side effects, apparently, was that she might be grumpy. They obviously didn't know her before the operation," Bella said with a laugh.

Chapter 20

Daphne wrapped her hands around Sparrow's small fingers, gently adjusting her grip on the fishing rod. She was trying to teach Sparrow the finer points of beach fishing, one of her favourite pastimes. Sparrow had expressed an interest in learning, so they could share the hobby together. However, much to Sparrow's frustration, Daphne's fishing rods were proving far too big for her to manage.

Daphne was valiantly trying to supress her laughter at the hilarious results of Sparrow's attempts at casting. It was like watching one of those funniest home video movies, she decided, as Sparrow ended up each time with either a hook entangled in her hair, the bait flying off the hook or the line tangling. Eventually, after a rare successful cast, Sparrow gave a shriek of excitement when she felt something large tug on her line. She eagerly reeled in her catch, only to find a huge clump of seaweed hanging from her hook.

Visibly deflated, Sparrow stomped across the sand to sit on the picnic blanket. She pointedly ignored Daphne, who gave up trying not to laugh. Giggling uncontrollably, she walked over to Sparrow, lay the beach rod on the sand and sat down.

"Don't get so upset, honey. We just need to get you a smaller rod next time we're in town."

Sparrow pouted, unwilling to be so quickly mollified. "I just thought it would be nice to share this with you because it is something you enjoy so much."

"Well, you don't have to fish. If you wanted to, we could just come down to the beach and I could fish while you... read or something."

Daphne repositioned herself behind Sparrow, drawing her small body between her legs and back against her chest.

"What is it about fishing that you love so much?" Sparrow asked, leaning back into her embrace.

Daphne rested her chin gently on Sparrow's head and stared out at the ocean, thinking about her response. "I have always loved the ocean, ever since I was a kid. If I'm distressed, or upset, I find that just sitting watching the movement of the waves soothes me like nothing else. When I'm fishing it's just me; me and the sea. It's not about what I catch. Mostly I throw them back. It's just about being part of the rhythm of the ocean. It allows me to think, clear my mind and get centred again."

Sparrow tilted her head back, looking up at her lover with a smile. "Remember you told me when we first started going out together, that everything happens for a reason?"

Daphne nodded.

"Well, that's why my trying to fish is such a disaster."

Daphne frowned, "I'm not sure I understand..."

Sparrow sat up, turned and faced her. "The main thing about fishing for you is solitude. You said you get centred, just you and the ocean. That is incredibly important. If I join you, then that all changes and it becomes just another thing we share."

"But it's important that we share things, isn't it?" Daphne asked, trying to understand.

"Of course it is, but not at the expense of something that is such a basic need for you. We can share lots of things, but we also need to remember that we need our alone time as well. One of those things for you is fishing. It's your alone time. It's that simple."

Daphne pondered what Sparrow was saying, and realised she was right.

"So, you don't mind if I go fishing by myself?" she asked cautiously.

Sparrow tilted up and kissed Daphne. "Of course not, especially if you bring fresh fish home sometimes."

"Just say the word and you can have all the fresh fish I can catch you."

Sparrow stretched. "Feel like a swim?" she asked.

"Why not?" Daphne agreed. "I could do with cooling off."

Sparrow rose, looking around the small cove to ensure that it was deserted, then removed her shirt and shorts. Daphne tossed her swimming costume to her, then leant back to watch her change, a lazy smile on her face. Sparrow threw the costume back, smirked, then slowly began removing her underwear.

Daphne bolted upright, mesmerised, as Sparrow slowly removed her panties and bra.

"Come over here, you brazen hussy," she demanded huskily.

Sparrow grinned. "Nope, you want me, you gotta catch me." With that, she ran the short distance across the beach and plunged quickly into the water.

Throwing caution to the wind, Daphne stood, tore her clothes off and ran down the beach, diving in to join Sparrow in the ocean.

"Damn, but that water's cold," she gasped, shaking water out of her eyes as she surfaced next to the naked body of her lover.

Sparrow placed her hands on Daphne's shoulders and wrapped her legs around her waist.

"Is that any warmer?" She grinned cheekily.

Daphne could feel the heat of Sparrow's centre pressed against her abdomen. The contrast of the heat from Sparrow's body pressed against the chill of her skin made Daphne dizzy with desire. Crushing her mouth to Sparrow's, she placed her hands under her buttocks, supporting the smaller woman. Feeling Sparrow beginning to move rhythmically against her, Daphne's toes curled as a flash of desire streaked through her. Lifting Sparrow a little higher, Daphne captured a rosy nipple in her mouth, relishing Sparrow's gasp as her warm tongue enclosed the pointed flesh. Slowly, Daphne moved her fingers to Sparrow's centre. Sparrow leant back in her arms, drops of water beading her body, desire evident in her eyes.

"Kiss me, Daphne," Sparrow panted.

Pulling Sparrow's body back to her own, Daphne captured her mouth once again and felt Sparrow shudder against her as waves of contractions rippled around her fingers.

Gentling her kiss, Daphne cradled Sparrow in her arms. The women held each other for several minutes, gently swaying in the water. Daphne closed her eyes, dazed once again by the feelings that swept over her.

"Hey, why the tears? What's wrong?" Sparrow asked, wiping Daphne's cheeks with her thumbs.

Daphne shook her head, swamped by a myriad of emotions. She wasn't sure whether she wanted to run a million miles away, or to stay and hold Sparrow like this forever.

"Daph, what is it? Tell me," Sparrow murmured, stroking her face

Daphne shook her head, gasping, "I can't explain it...I just feel..."

Sparrow kissed her gently. "I know, I feel it as well. It's a little overwhelming, isn't it, love?"

Daphne lowered Sparrow back into the water. "I didn't expect this. I had my life all mapped out and then you walked in and...nothing's familiar anymore, everything's changed." Running her hand over her face, she looked at her lover. "I don't know if I can do this. I just need some space to deal with it all, Sparrow," she admitted quietly.

Sparrow's face showed her dread at Daphne's words. Resting her head against Daphne's chest, she fought to stay calm. "It's okay, honey, we can work this out. There's no rush. We can take all the time you need."

Nodding mutely as she heard the edge of panic in Sparrow's voice, Daphne closed her eyes, feeling the growing apprehension and uncertainty fracture the intimacy they had just shared.

Slowly, they waded back to the shore and gathered their towels and clothing. They turned away to dry themselves and dress, then silently packed away their picnic basket and fishing gear.

As they trudged back towards the car, Sparrow looked across at Daphne's set expression.

"Did I tell you that Bella is having some friends over tomorrow for afternoon tea? There's a small group of us going and I was wondering if you had anything planned with Pat?" she asked quietly.

"I haven't spoken to Pat for a week or so. I have no idea what she's up to," Daphne said brusquely.

"You could give her a call. She might be glad of the company," Sparrow suggested with a hesitant smile.

Reaching the car, Daphne unlocked the boot and placed their gear inside. At the driver's door, she stopped to look across at Sparrow. "You don't need to manage me. I am perfectly capable of contacting my friends without any prompting."

Clenching her jaw, Sparrow got into the car and busied herself with her seatbelt.

"I'm not trying to manage you, Daphne. I'm just..." she hesitated, confused at how suddenly everything had spiralled out of control.

"Just what?" Daphne asked, wrenching the car into gear.

Sparrow leant against her seat and closed her eyes, trying to keep her breathing even.

"Nothing. Let's just go home," she said quietly, turning away to look out the window.

Turning the radio on loudly, Daphne drove them back to the village.

At Sparrow's cottage, Daphne quickly helped collect her picnic basket and beach gear. After dropping them at the doorstep, she turned to walk back to her car.

"Daphne," Sparrow said, laying her hand on Daphne's arm. "Don't leave like this. Come inside. Let's talk. Please."

Daphne shook her head. The earlier surge of anger she felt had dissipated, leaving her feeling confused, guilty and desperate to escape.

"I can't, Sparrow. I really need to go home and be by myself. I'm sorry I ruined our day." Gazing at her sadly, Daphne gently touched Sparrow's face. "Please try and understand. I really do want to try and make this work. I feel like everything's happened so fast and I just need some time to work it all out."

Sparrow nodded, her shoulders slumped. "Sure," she said with the ghost of a smile. "Give me a call when you are ready to talk."

Chapter 21

Tossing the magazine she had been trying to read onto the chair next to her bed, Meg looked around her large, sunny room. She had been moved to the rehab facility a week ago, where she'd immediately commenced an exercise regime with Casey, her young and, in Meg's opinion, far too enthusiastic physiotherapist. She had hoped that she would be allowed to go straight back to OWL's from the hospital, but Dr Wilcox was reluctant. "I just want to be sure, Meg. Ten days in the rehab under Casey's guidance and then, all being well, you can go home."

Meg had received regular visits from OWL's residents, but despite all of the attention, she was fed up. She hated feeling dependent, her scar was starting to itch and she desperately wanted to go home and take control of her life again.

"Morning, Meg"

Jolted from her funk, Meg realised Bella and Pat were standing in her doorway. Her delight at seeing them was tempered by her dismay that, once again, Allie was not with them. Smiling through her disappointment, she welcomed them into her room.

"Oh am I glad to see you two," she declared. "I am nearly going crazy with boredom. I almost wish Casey was here today so I could have someone to snipe at."

Bella moved the magazine from the chair next to the bed and sat down as Pat brought the other chair over alongside it.

"So have you any news on when they are going to evict you from here?" Pat joked.

"Jenny's coming to see me tomorrow and I am hoping she'll tell me then. I just want to get back home. I mean, they are so kind here and are looking after me beautifully, but…"

"It's not home," Bella finished, taking Meg's hand.

Meg nodded, suddenly aware of the lump in her throat.

"So," she said, taking a deep breath, "enough about me. What's happening at home?"

Bella and Pat filled her in on the events of the last couple of days. Meg was shocked to hear about the rift between Daphne and Sparrow.

"Oh no, they can't let that go! They're so right together. I know I thought it was an odd pairing when they first became involved, but sometimes you just need to follow your heart. They seemed to be making it work, and it was wonderful to see the two of them so happy."

Pat shrugged. "Well, Sparrow won't be trifled with, and I have to admire her determination. Until Daphne decides that she wants to commit to a relationship, Sparrow is adamant she won't have anything to do with her. She's not the slightest bit interested in a 'friends with benefits' arrangement. She's prepared to accept a friendship if a committed relationship is not an option, but she's drawn a line in the sand and isn't backing away from it.

Bella shook her head. "We aren't sure that giving Daphne all the power is such a good idea, but Sparrow seems to believe it will make her honestly assess what she wants. In view of her past experiences with relationships, it's causing Sparrow a world of heartbreak, but we we're giving her as much support as we can."

"Daphne can't run away, or just push this one under the carpet. If she wants a life with Sparrow, she has to stop being an idiot and sort herself out. I have to admit, Daphne has been totally miserable over the past week, so maybe Sparrow does have the right idea," Pat admitted.

Meg stared off into the distance. "Daphne needs to realise that once in a lifetime someone comes into your life that you are meant to be with, and if you let them go, nothing will ever be quite right again," she said thoughtfully.

Pat met Bella's eyes, and an unspoken message passed between them.

"Darling, would you do me a favour and get my jacket out of the car? I'm feeling a bit chilly in here," Bella asked.

"I can give you my sweater..." Pat offered.

"No, *cara*, just go grab my jacket. It's on the backseat."

"No problem. I'll be back in a flash," Pat called, heading obediently for the door.

<hr />

Bella turned back to Meg and gently took her hand.

Meg linked their fingers. "How is she?" she asked quietly.

"It's hard to know, Meg. You know what Allie's like. She refuses to talk to us about anything remotely connected to you. On one level she seems fine, but..." Bella shrugged.

"She hasn't been to see me; she hasn't called. I've tried ringing her but it just goes to message bank. I know you said she is angry with me for not telling her about my symptoms.

I agree, I should have done, but that's me, that's just the way I am. I don't understand, Bella, is she angry that I survived?" Meg asked sadly.

"She feels betrayed, betrayed and terribly hurt, *cara*. You put yourself at huge personal risk and she feels you either couldn't trust her enough, or you didn't care enough about her to let her know what was going on."

Meg laughed incredulously. "Didn't care enough about her? Doesn't she know? I've loved that woman since the first moment I saw her at that damned party forty years ago. I've never stopped loving her…and I probably never will." Meg closed her eyes as tears threatened, her anguish evident in her voice.

Bella leant forward, grasping Meg's hand tighter. "Then tell her, Meg. You said it yourself, sometimes someone walks into your life that you are just meant to be with."

"It's a bit hard to tell her if she won't talk to me. Besides, I know she loves me as a friend, but that's all. Do you know last month we were seconds away from kissing?" Bella's eyes widened and she leant in as Meg continued, "We got interrupted, but the shock on Allie's face when we pulled apart told me everything I needed to know. She could barely even look at me." Meg shook her head. "If friendship is all I have with her, then I don't want to risk losing it by making a total fool of myself."

Bella threw up her hands in frustration. "Meg, for a sensible, educated woman you can be very dense. Trust me, I know what loves looks like and I see it very clearly in both of you."

Meg sat, absorbing Bella's words. "Well if she loves me so much, where the hell is she?" she sulked, picking at the edge of her coverlet.

"Here's your jacket, honey," Pat announced, walking back into the room.

Bella stood and took the jacket. "Thank you, darling. I think we should probably get going now. Meg looks tired and we don't want to wear her out."

"Oh, all right then, sure." Pat said, somewhat confused. "You all right, Meg?"

Meg smiled. "I could probably do with a nap. I honestly can't believe how much I'm sleeping. One minute I feel fine and then the next I can hardly keep my eyes open."

Bella bent to give Meg a farewell kiss. Placing a hand on her cheek, she murmured quietly, "Think about our conversation. Love is too important not to fight for."

"Meg, as soon as the doctor gives you the all clear to come home, let us know and we'll come and pick you up," Pat reminded her.

"Thank you so much. That would be wonderful. Though I think I will be so happy to get out of here I could probably skip home." Meg laughed.

———— ⬦ ————

As they walked away from the hospital, Pat nudged Bella. "You didn't really need your jacket did you?"

Bella smiled and squeezed her arm. "Sorry, darling, I wanted to talk to Meg about Allie and..."

Pat held the car door open for her. "Yep, I get it. Girl talk... So what did you find out?"

"Well, we were right. Meg does love Allie, has done for forty years. However, she is adamant that Allie doesn't return her feelings."

"Well, I can't say I'm that surprised," Pat responded, as she eased the car into traffic. "I don't think Allie is aware of it either! I mean, how can you love someone and not admit it? Honestly, I don't know why everyone makes it so hard. Love is love; it's not damned rocket science. Meg, Allie and Daphne all need a swift kick up the backside. The three of them have the most wonderful chance in front of them, and they are all dithering around the edge, too scared to jump in. Honestly, it makes me so cross."

"Imagine if you had been too scared to pursue me all those years ago. Just think what we would have missed," Bella agreed.

"Yeah, and you know how scared I was, but what I felt for you was bigger than my fear. There was nothing and no-one, not your father, brothers or whole extended family, that could have persuaded me to walk away from you."

"You've always been my champion." Bella reached over, linking their hands.

Pat glanced across at her, bringing Bella's hand to her lips. "And you, my darling, have always been my lady."

Bella laughed and suddenly it was as if all the worries of the last months slipped away. Pat was right, love was the greatest gift two people could find, and as she watched her driving, she saw once again the vibrant young woman she had fallen in love with forty-five years ago. They may have gotten older and greyer and their bodies may carry the scars of their lives, but she knew that in their hearts they were just as young as they had been all those years ago.

Chapter 22

AFTER MORNING TEA AT PAT and Bella's, Sparrow walked slowly home, deep in thought. Despite giving her the requested time and space since the episode at the beach several weeks ago, Daphne appeared to be no closer to resolving her problems. They had seen each other twice, both of which had been awkward, leaving Sparrow no clearer regarding Daphne's intentions. In desperation, she had spoken of her fears and frustration to Pat and Bella, both of whom had urged her to maintain her distance.

"If she wants you, then she is going to need to make the commitment." Bella had been firm.

"I still don't understand what she's scared of," Pat had said crossly. "As far as I can see, all this talk of needing time is just an excuse." Seeing Sparrow's rising panic, Pat had smiled, quickly reassuring her. "I don't doubt for a moment that she loves you, Sparrow, but she won't listen to me. As far as I'm concerned, she needs a damned wake-up call."

Sparrow continued to mull over the conversation as she made her way home, stopping suddenly as Pat's words replayed in her head. She was right; Daphne didn't need Sparrow to be compliant and understanding. What Daphne needed was a shock, and Sparrow was finally in the mood to give it to her.

Empowered by her resolution, she walked briskly to Daphne's cottage and knocked firmly on the door.

"Sparrow," Daphne said in surprise, standing hesitantly in the doorway.

Sparrow looked directly at her. "There's something I need to say," she said bluntly. "I know you're having problems coming to terms with our relationship, but I can't make the decision for you; we are either worth it, or we aren't. I believe we've been given something special, another chance that neither of us was expecting. I know that this relationship is something I want and I know how I feel about you. What you need to do is figure out your feelings and what you want. Just don't take too long, Daphne, because I won't wait forever."

With a last look at Daphne's stunned expression, Sparrow turned and walked away.

Chapter 23

LESLIE BARLOW'S BIRTHDAY PARTY WAS in full swing, laughter and soft music filling the games room. Daphne stood talking to several women about an upcoming fishing trip they were planning. A sixth sense made her look up just as Sparrow arrived with Helen Macintosh. In a dove grey silk dress, her shoulders covered with a shawl that she had obviously embroidered herself, Sparrow was beautiful. Their eyes met, and Sparrow smiled coolly as she and Helen walked over to join a group on the other side of the room.

"So what do you think, Daph, are you happy to do it that way?" one of the women in her group asked.

"Sorry...what?" Daphne asked distractedly, still watching Sparrow and Helen out of the corner of her eye.

"The transport; if we take Gail and Mary's SUV..."

"Yeah, whatever," she agreed hurriedly. "Sorry, I've got to go and catch up with someone."

Excusing herself, Daphne walked over to join Bella and Pat. They too had seen Sparrow walk in and were both keenly watching Daphne's reaction. As Daphne sat in the chair next to Pat, she gave a deep sigh.

Fixing her with a long look, Pat motioned towards Sparrow. "So, what are you going to do about her?"

Daphne's focus remained directed at the women standing with Sparrow. Before she had a chance to respond, peals of laughter arose from the group and Daphne winced, her gut clenching at the way Helen possessively placed an arm around Sparrow to whisper into her ear.

Leaning in to better make her point, Pat said, "It's simple, Daphne. You either want to be with her, or you don't. Just stop messing about and make up your mind."

Nodding resolutely at her friends, Daphne stood. "Well, I'm damned if I'm going to stand by and watch Helen push me out of the way." Handing her drink to Pat, she took a deep breath.

Smiling, Pat took the proffered glass "Remember what I said. Just tell her what's in your heart."

Sparrow turned and Daphne's eyes locked on to her as she drew closer. Neither appeared conscious of anyone else in the room. Standing this close to Sparrow again made Daphne feel like a tongue-tied fourteen-year-old. Everything she meant to say flew right out of her head.

Helen moved into Daphne's sight, blocking her path to Sparrow and bringing her resolutely back to earth.

"Daphne, I didn't think you would be here tonight," Helen drawled with a condescending smile.

Taking a deep breath, Daphne eyeballed Helen. As much as she wanted to wipe the superior look off her face, Daphne forced a smile, glancing over Helen's shoulder at Sparrow.

"If you don't mind, I have something I need to discuss with Sparrow…alone," she said quietly.

Helen moved into Daphne's space. "Frankly, I don't think Sparrow has anything she wants to say to you, so it might be less embarrassing for you if you just walk away."

Sparrow placed her hand on Helen's arm, drawing her away from Daphne. "I'm sorry, Helen, but I think it's important that Daphne and I talk."

Helen spoke softly. "You don't have to talk to her, you know. If you are uncomfortable here, we can just go back to my place."

Sparrow smiled briefly at Daphne, indicating that she would be with her in a moment, then turned back to Helen apologetically.

"I'm sorry, Helen," she said softly. "I am fond of you as a friend, but as lovers it would never work. Daphne and I need to sort out our relationship. Please try and understand."

Letting out a sigh, Helen nodded sadly, leant into Sparrow and kissed her on the cheek. "You're a very special woman, and for what it's worth, I hope the two of you work it out. If you ever change your mind, though," she whispered, "you know where I am."

Sparrow turned and stepped towards Daphne and together they walked into the garden. The warm evening carried the scent of roses and night jasmine, and music from the party spilled softly into the garden. Sparrow regarded Daphne carefully for a moment, a hint of defiance in her eyes.

"Well, what is it you want to discuss?" she finally asked.

Recognising the hurt etched on Sparrow's face, Daphne felt her heart constrict. "I have been such a damned fool,

Sparrow. I've spent so much time alone over the past ten years, telling myself that I never wanted to be hurt again, that I forgot what living was all about. Then you came into my life and I wanted you so much it scared me to death. You seemed so sure about everything; it all seemed so easy for you. I ran because I was scared, because my old familiar life, as dreary as it was, was safe." Close to tears, Daphne looked across at Sparrow. "But I've missed you so much and been so damned miserable these last weeks..." Straightening her shoulders and taking a deep breath, she continued, "Well, if this is what happens when I play it safe, then to hell with it. I love you and I swear, if you can forgive me, I will never run out on you again."

Sparrow shook her head in frustration, pulling her shawl around her shoulders. "Easy? You think it was easy for me? Do you seriously believe I wasn't scared? Just because I seemed sure didn't mean I was. I spent whole days wondering if being in a relationship with you, or anyone for that matter, was the right thing to do. But despite all my doubts and fears, what kept me going, was that I believed in us." Sparrow's voice broke. "You have no idea how incredibly hurt I was when you pushed me away, because it meant that you didn't share that belief. I felt so rejected, so humiliated, and so alone."

"Well, I notice that Helen seems to be more than happy to keep you company," Daphne sulked.

Sparrow put her hands on her hips, anger lacing her voice. "Yes, you're right. Helen is wonderfully entertaining and she seems to have no problem with committing herself to a relationship, especially with me. However, it seems to have escaped your notice that Helen, as attentive as she is, is not the person I love."

Daphne felt her heart race as their eyes met. "You still love me, even after the way I behaved?" she asked hesitantly, her breath catching at the enormity of her question.

Sparrow's anger crumbled at the love in Daphne's eyes. She reached for Daphne's hand, clasping it in both of hers as she clutched it to her chest.

"Honey, loving someone is like a deal with the devil; there's good and bad, but whatever happens, you can't change what you feel. I still can't believe that I've been given another chance at love. Yes, of course I love you, or I wouldn't be out here having this conversation with you." Reaching for Daphne's other hand, she smiled. "Let's take it with both hands and never let go."

Daphne bent and kissed her, and as their lips touched, a warm glow ran through her body. Breaking from their kiss with a contented sigh, Sparrow looked back towards the games room.

"Listen," she said softly as the strains of Chely Wright's "What If We Fly" floated into the garden, "I think they may be playing our song."

Daphne put her arms around Sparrow, drawing her close, relishing the feel of Sparrow's body against hers. Their bodies moved in time to the music, pausing only to exchange soft kisses and murmur their love for each other.

"Do you think anyone would mind if we quietly left this party and headed home?" Daphne finally asked.

"I'm sure they would all much prefer that to finding us naked in the garden, which is what will happen very soon if I don't get you somewhere private," Sparrow breathed, running her hands along Daphne's back.

Daphne tilted Sparrow's face up and placed a tender kiss on her lips. "Then take me home and let me show you how much I've missed you."

Chapter 24

ALLIE SAMPLED A PIECE OF one of the macadamia prawn cakes she had set to cool on the kitchen bench and nodded her approval. To her delight, it was even better than the recipe had suggested. Placing the golden cakes on a plate, she covered them with Glad Wrap to take to Bella and Pat's later. As she searched for room in the fridge, she glanced over the multitude of dishes ready to be stacked in the freezer, evidence of her marathon cooking spree over the last few days.

Allie was still trying to process the 'almost kiss'. Now with the aftermath of Meg's heart attack, she was feeling so completely distracted that her only protection was to immerse herself in her kitchen. While she diced, blended, measured and created, she found herself able to think more clearly and allowed the routine of her craft to soothe her enough to regain a sense of control. Now, more than ever, she clung to that sense of balance, because everything felt as if it was in total free fall.

Since Meg's heart attack, she had hidden herself away at home, not wanting to talk to anyone, refusing all invitations and visitors. Finally, this week, a very determined Bella had refused to be turned away.

"Allie, Pat and I are worried about you and we insist that you come to dinner," Bella had said, sitting at Allie's kitchen table sharing a pot of tea. Looking at her friend, she'd gently wiped away a smudge of flour from Allie's cheek. "You can't keep hiding in your kitchen."

"It's the only thing that helps, Bella. I keep telling myself that if I keep doing what I love, a sense of order will take over and I will be back in control and able to think rationally about it all." Looking around her kitchen at the myriad of pots and pans bubbling on the stove, Allie had let out a big sigh.

Bella had shaken her head. "There is an Italian expression, *cibo nutre il vostro stomaco, amici nutrono la tua anima*, that roughly translates as 'food feeds your stomach, but friends feed your soul'." Taking Allie's hand in both of hers, Bella had leant in. "Come for dinner, bring some of the wonderful product of all this confusion and let Pat and I help you through this. It's only us, Allie."

Allie knew that Bella was right. She did need to be around the people who cared for her, who might be able to help her make sense of this mess. She also knew she needed to do something before Meg's return to the village in the next few days.

While cleaning up her kitchen, she once again tried to sort through the tangle of emotions taunting her. She wanted to be happy that the surgery had been successful and that Meg had recovered so well, but a greater part of her emotions were stuck on the fact that the heart attack should never have happened in the first place. That because of Meg's stubborn pride and inability to trust her...

There it was again, the one thing she kept coming back to: despite everything they'd been through together over the last forty years, Meg had endangered her own life rather than trust Allie to help her. *Well, damn her*, she thought, throwing the dishcloth in the sink with force. She was done with fretting about Meg.

Allie looked around her kitchen. Bella was right; she had hidden herself away for far too long. It was time she got out, relaxed and enjoyed an evening with her two good friends.

Chapter 25

BELLA FINISHED PREPARING THE SALADS and placed them carefully in the fridge. Looking out the kitchen window, she watched Pat fire up the barbeque. Complete with her "Kiss the Cook" apron, Pat was a picture of efficient organisation as she laid out her barbeque utensils. It had been such a hot day that they'd decided an al fresco sunset meal under the pergola would be ideal. Pat had set up several citronella candles around the table to keep the mosquitos at bay and their flickering flames cast an inviting light over the tablecloth and place settings.

Pat came back inside and walked over to the fridge to grab a cold beer.

"You need help with anything, sweetie?" she asked.

Bella finished wiping down the benches. "No, *cara*, the salads are made, the potatoes have been precooked and are ready for the barbeque and the steaks are marinating in the fridge."

Pat took a long drink of her beer. "I am just waiting for the barbeque to heat up a little more, and then I'll drop in the potatoes."

Hearing the doorbell chime, Bella walked down the hallway and opened the door for Allie.

"Welcome, Allie," she greeted, motioning her into the cool hallway. Taking Allie's proffered plate and placing it on the hall table, Bella enveloped her in a long hug and then kissed both her cheeks. "We are so glad you came."

Allie returned the hug and kisses. "So am I," she replied, smiling fondly.

Pat joined them, also wrapping Allie in a welcoming hug. "I suspect, knowing the love of my life as I do, that you weren't given much of a choice." She grinned.

Laughing, Allie picked up the plate and followed her friends into the living room.

"No, you were right. I've been hiding myself away and ignoring my friends. It's high time I rejoined the world. If anything, I am grateful that you both care so much about me," she confessed.

Taking the plate from Allie, Bella peeked under the cover. "Does this need heating up? What is it that smells so delicious?"

"Macadamia prawn cakes and yes, you can heat them, but I thought it might be better to eat them cold." Digging into her bag, Allie brought out a small bottle. "I've also brought some dressing we can have with them."

While Bella transferred the cakes to a serving platter, Allie accepted a glass of wine from Pat and followed her out to the pergola, where she sat at the small patio table as Pat dropped potatoes into the barbeque.

"This is such a beautiful area now. The two of you have done a wonderful job."

Pat smiled. "Well, Bella had this idea in her head of what she wanted this area to look like. I'm just so glad I was able to create the reality for her. It's been a real haven for her since she's been sick."

With her glass of wine in hand, Allie relaxed back in her chair and watched Pat at the barbeque. Obviously happy with the progress of the potatoes, she carefully placed the three marinated steaks on the grill. The sizzle and aroma made Allie aware of just how hungry she was. Her stomach growled as Pat turned the steaks and prepared the potatoes for serving.

"So, *andiamo*," Bella exclaimed as she carried platters of food out from the kitchen and placed them on the table. "Let's eat."

As Bella and Pat sang the praises of the prawn cakes and the wine began to take effect, Allie felt herself truly relaxing. The succulent meal and laughter at Pat's endless stories made her realise how much she had missed the company of true friends.

"Oh, I don't think I could eat another mouthful," Allie declared several hours later as she finished her dessert. "That was a truly wonderful meal."

"It's hard to beat a good old Aussie barbeque," Pat agreed.

"Or a wonderful Italian tiramasu," Bella reminded her.

"Tonight's meal was indeed the perfect blending of cultures," Pat announced with mock formality. She rose to clear the table, brushing off Allie's offer of assistance. "No, you stay and keep Bella company. I have this under control."

"So, *cara*, tell me, how you are doing?" Bella asked quietly, as Pat busied herself with clean up in the kitchen.

Allie took a deep breath and gathered her thoughts.

"I have no idea," she admitted with a half laugh. "I've cooked enough food to feed the village for a month in the hope that it will somehow help me get my emotions in order, but although it has worked in the past, all it's done this time is fill up my freezer and given me indigestion. I'm still no closer to resolving how I feel. I am so tired of being angry with Meg. One minute I want to march right up to her and tell her what I think, and the next...I'm terrified of seeing her and want to run away. None of it seems to make any sense."

"Are you still angry with her for not trusting you?"

Allie nodded, sipping her wine. "I was at first; now I'm just sad. If she had told me what she was going through I could have helped her, but she refused. I can only assume that she cares so little for me that she preferred to risk dying," she said bitterly.

Bella looked up to see Pat standing quietly in the doorway, listening. At Pat's subtle nod, Bella leant in closer to her friend.

"You know, trust is a strange thing, Allie. It takes time to develop and it is incredibly fragile. If you trust someone, you have to admit your vulnerability and in some situations that is not easy to do."

"Obviously it is far too hard for Meg to admit," Allie snapped.

Looking across to Pat for support, Bella tried again. "Remember when I was going through the chemotherapy treatment and Pat and I were having problems with her trying to protect me?"

Allie nodded cautiously, not sure where this conversation was going. "Yes, we talked at length about it the day I came for lunch."

"She was so terrified of anything happening to me that rather than risk me not coping, she just removed everything and everyone from around me, in the hope of keeping me safe."

"Which, I remember, infuriated you," Allie said seriously.

"Exactly, because I felt as if Pat didn't trust me enough to tell her if I wasn't coping."

Allie frowned, thinking about Bella's words. "So what you're saying is that Meg thought she was keeping me safe by keeping her illness from me?"

Pat took her seat next to Allie. "Sometimes it's impossible to know what to do when you are in a situation like that. The last thing she would have wanted to do was hurt you."

"But that's ridiculous," Allie retorted. "It's not the same thing at all… I mean, you and Bella are in love with each other."

"Yes, we are, and sometimes, that's what people do when they're in love," Bella quietly confirmed, her eyes never leaving Allie's face.

Allie's eyes widened and she felt her heart stutter as she took in the meaning of her friend's words.

Drawing her chair closer to Allie, Bella put an arm around her. "Has it really never occurred to you before?"

Allie sat stunned. Suddenly so many things fell into place, the realisation leaving her breathless.

Shaking her head, she whispered, "She loves me? I mean, as in…real love?"

"*Si.*" Bella smiled. "Very much as in real love."

Allie looked at her friends in confusion. "Wait, how did you two know?'

"Sweetie, I think the only person who didn't know, or at least didn't acknowledge it, was you," said Pat with a smile

Bella watched Allie carefully. "The six million dollar question is, do you love Meg?"

Allie sat back in her chair. Her head was spinning; she couldn't seem to grasp any solid thoughts. Looking back,

Allie found it inconceivable that she had not realised Meg's feelings for her.

"I...I'm not sure. I don't know," she stuttered. "It never occurred to me that she loved me...not like that. I mean, she could have any woman she wanted." Allie stared out at the garden, remembering. "I was crazy about her when we first met," she began softly. "We talked about it once, but somehow we both decided that we would make better friends than lovers. I just pushed my feelings for her away after that. I guess I buried them so deep that I was able to ignore them."

"But they didn't completely disappear?" Bella asked with a smile.

Allie closed her eyes. "But...why wouldn't she say something to me?"

"You've had forty years of hiding those feeling, Allie," Bella said gently. "If you couldn't admit them to yourself, how was Meg to know?"

Bella and Pat watched as Allie struggled to comprehend this revelation.

"Are you sure?" she whispered.

Bella smiled. "You don't have to believe us, Allie. Look into your heart; the answer's right there."

Pat took Allie's hands and gently pulled her to her feet to envelop her in a hug. "You don't have to work it all out now," she whispered quietly. "It's a lot to take in and you need time to let it settle. You know we're here if you need us."

Allie choked back a sob, her emotions threatening to completely overwhelm her, then hugged them both tightly.

"I'm sorry, I think I need to go home and think about all this. Do you mind?" she asked, already heading for the door, gathering her bag and jacket.

"I'd be happy to drive you," Pat offered, following Allie to the front door.

"No, the walk will do me good, maybe help clear my head. Thank you so much for dinner. I'll call you tomorrow," she promised, waving good night.

Allie walked home in a daze. Twenty minutes later, she was surprised to find herself sitting in her own kitchen with a half-drunk cup of tea in her hand and no real awareness of how she got there. Thinking back over her conversation with Bella and Pat, she kept coming to the same realisation.

"She loves me," Allie said aloud. "She's always loved me. I've just been too stupid to see it."

Closing her eyes, she let the words sink in, feeling the mixture of emotions they elicited. Resting her head in her hands, Allie sighed deeply.

"Oh, Meg, what the hell am I going to do now?"

Chapter 26

MEG WAS THINKING ABOUT HER future. Dressed, and with her bag packed, she sat on her bed waiting for Jenny Wilcox to discharge her. After spending so many days desperate to go home, now that the time was finally here, she found herself strangely reluctant to leave the safe confines of the room. She kept telling herself it was because she was nervous about her health, but the reality was that she was more afraid of what lay ahead.

Jenny knocked as she entered and Meg looked up, studying her closely.

"So, finally ready to get out of here?" Jenny asked.

"Yes. I thought it would never happen," Meg sighed, fiddling with her watch. "Pat and Bella should be here soon to collect me and then I'll be out of your hair."

Seeing Meg's agitation, Jenny put her stethoscope to her ears. "Just once more, for old time's sake?" she prompted with a smile, indicating the stethoscope.

Rolling her eyes and grumbling about over-protectiveness, Meg opened her shirt for the examination. When she was satisfied, Jenny removed the stethoscope and sat next to Meg.

"Well, it all seems to be perfect physically, so you should have no fears about a relapse. The chance of another heart attack is very slight. You are in excellent shape for a woman of your age and if you keep up the exercise regime that Casey has prepared for you, you should have many more years of good health. However, I will be insisting on check-ups at six-month intervals, just to make sure." She looked at Meg sternly. "I know we've had this conversation before, but I'll tell you again. If there are any symptoms at all, you must come and see me immediately. You simply cannot afford to ignore any signs. They happen for a reason."

Meg coloured. She understood how foolish she had been by not bringing her symptoms to the attention of medical staff. Whilst that embarrassed her, it paled in comparison to the impact it had had on her relationship with Allie. Nodding, she promised to let Jenny know the minute she felt any unusual twinges.

At that moment, Pat and Bella strolled through the door, ready to escort her home. Once again her eyes flittered past them, and once again she battled disappointment when she realised they were alone.

"So," grinned Pat, "now can we take this old broad home with us?"

Jenny laughed at the glare Meg directed at Pat. "Yes, she's been cluttering up this room for far too long. Take her home and try and make sure she stays out of trouble."

"Chance would be a fine thing," Pat quipped, rolling her eyes.

Standing, Meg poked Pat in the ribs whilst piercing her with a familiar glare. "In case you had forgotten already, I'm in this room, you know, and there is no need to be quite so rude."

Bella shook her head. "Take no notice, Meg; we're delighted to be taking you home. It's going to be wonderful to have you back with us all again."

A nurse appeared with a wheelchair, and Meg groaned. "Oh for goodness sake! After all the rehab I've done over the last three weeks and you want to wheel me out of here?"

Jenny laughed. "Medical policy, Meg. Only way out the front door is in one of these."

Meg sat in the chair, and Pat grabbed the handles, laughing. "This may be the only chance I ever get to push Meg around."

Waving goodbye to the rehab staff, they made their way to the car park. As Pat attempted to help her into the car, Meg turned on her.

"Honestly, Pat, I think I can get into a car by myself!" Seeing Pat's reaction and the shock on Bella's face, Meg closed her eyes in embarrassment and sighed. "I'm sorry, that was uncalled for. I know you're trying to help. It's just that I'm so tired of feeling like an invalid. Being in hospital for weeks and having people always doing everything for me has worn me to a frazzle. I have never been good at accepting help, and I am still getting used to this level of dependence."

"Well, I think you might need to keep working on it," Bella admonished. "Being able to reach out and ask when you need something is a lesson I thought you would have learnt by now."

Meg quietly settled into the back seat, struggling to think of an appropriate response to Bella's sharp comment before deciding to let it go. Being defensive with her friends was not going to help matters.

Bella turned to face Meg. "Talking of asking for help, Allie came to dinner with us the other night. We had an... interesting evening."

Meg watched as Bella glanced at Pat, who remained steadfastly focussed on the road ahead; she was aware of an unspoken message underlying the words.

"Interesting how?" she asked gruffly.

"Let's talk about this some more when we get you home; we're nearly there," replied Bella.

As the car drew closer to the village turnoff, Meg's unease about seeing Allie escalated. She had been mulling over what Bella had said, but was still no clearer about her next step. She suspected that Allie's absence from the visitor's list was a pretty clear confirmation that Allie was still not talking to her. In fact, the more time that passed with no word from her, the more Meg truly worried that there may not even be a friendship worth salvaging.

As Pat turned the car into the driveway leading to OWL's Haven, Meg sat back, stunned. All the way along the driveway were handmade signs welcoming her home. Seeing Pat's grin in the rear vision mirror, Meg shook her head in disbelief. When they pulled up outside her cottage, Meg was amazed to see the crowd of residents waiting to greet her.

Turning to her, Bella smiled. "Are you ready for this?"

Meg scanned the expectant faces. The one face she was looking for was not there, but the others seemed genuinely pleased to have her home. Nodding her agreement, Meg climbed out of the car and into the arms of Daphne, who gave her an enthusiastic hug.

When Meg paled, Sparrow put her hand on Daphne's arm. "Honey, I know Meg's survived her heart attack, but I think she is probably still a little fragile."

Dropping her arms, Daphne stepped back in alarm. "Oh Lord, Meg, I'm so sorry. Are you all right? Did I hurt you?"

Meg took a deep breath and smiled at Daphne. "No, it was just what I needed after being away from you all for so long."

After several minutes of exuberant greetings, Bella and Pat ushered Meg into her cottage. Despite her reputation for hating any fuss and emotion, Meg found herself thoroughly enjoying the welcome and good wishes from so many friends and neighbours.

When the guest of honour began to visibly fade, Caro and Louise joined Bella and Pat in easing the crowd out the door.

"So, how are you feeling?" Louise asked, sitting on the sofa with Meg and Bella.

Meg smiled tiredly. "Honestly? I'm a little overwhelmed. I really didn't expect such a welcoming committee, but I am incredibly touched by their kindness."

"Well, Meg, we've always said we're a family," Caro said. "When something's wrong with one of us, the others will rally around. I don't think you realise just how many people care about you."

Meg, noticeably struggling with her emotions, was relieved when Bella redirected the conversation.

"Now, practical matters," she announced. "Several people have dropped off food for you. There's probably enough in your freezer to keep you going for six months. There are also the staples like eggs, bread and milk, all fresh and stacked away. Your sheets have been changed and the hot water service has been turned back on. Everything is as it was."

Meg rose and took Bella's hands. She felt a wave of emotion wash over her, aware of how far that statement was from the truth on so many levels.

"Thank you all so much for all you've done for me," she said shakily. "It's so wonderful to be in my own home again and surrounded by so many people who care."

Louise stood and kissed Meg on the cheek. "You know where we are; if there's anything you need just give us a call. The clinic nurse will drop in to see you each day while you settle back into your own routine. We'll catch up over the next couple of days and have a chat about medical matters. In the meantime, just relax and get plenty of rest."

She and Caro left, and Bella rose to put her arm around Meg's shoulders.

"You look very tired, my friend. Are you going to be able to manage here by yourself?"

Meg smiled wanly. "Yes, Bella. I just need to lie down for a while, but thank you again so much for your care and support."

"OK, we'll head off now, but give us a call when you wake up to let us know all is well. Please remember, if we don't hear from you, we'll be knocking on your door," she warned.

Meg closed the front door behind Bella and Pat, then walked into her bedroom and unpacked her bag. She was delighted to find that the room had been cleaned and tidied, but on her chest of drawers sat a broken frame with a note attached. She read:

Meg,

Welcome home!

Found this broken on the floor. Cleaned up the glass but wasn't sure if you wanted to keep the frame or get a new one.

Sally

As she turned the frame over, her breath caught in her throat as Allie's smiling face stared back at her. It was her favourite photo of the two of them, on holidays in Banff. Frowning, she wondered how it had been broken. Maybe she had dropped it the night of the heart attack. Her memories of that night were still not clear. Holding the photograph to her chest, she closed her eyes, anguished by the uncertainty between them.

"Oh, for heaven's sake, this is damned ridiculous. You are many things, Meg Sullivan, but a coward is not one of them," she admonished herself.

With newfound resolve, Meg brushed her hair and freshened her lipstick. She considered changing her clothes, but realised she was just delaying the inevitable. This had to be done and it had to be done now.

Meg marched out the front door and stared across the road at Allie's cottage. Her car wasn't in the carport and there was no sign of life, but Meg needed to go over and check for herself, just to make sure. Taking a steadying breath, she walked over and knocked loudly on the door. There was no response, so she knocked once again and called out. Finally, using her key, she let herself inside. As she opened the door and walked through the cottage, Meg instinctively knew that not only was Allie not there, but she hadn't been there for several days. In the kitchen, Meg was not surprised to have her thoughts confirmed.

"Hmmm, no milk, the stove is off and fridge is almost empty. You really aren't here, are you?" Meg said sadly into the empty space. Feeling defeated, she let herself out and slowly made her way back home.

Chapter 27

ALLIE SAT IN THE BEER garden of the local Berry pub, a crisp white wine in front of her, deep in her own thoughts. Two days earlier she'd packed a bag and left her cottage with no real idea of where she was going, just knowing that she had to leave before Meg returned. She'd booked into a local bed and breakfast and had spent her time walking along the beach, trying to redefine the last forty years and come to terms with the predicament she'd found herself in.

She knew she was running away, but she still hadn't formulated exactly how she felt about the discussion with Bella and Pat the previous week. She'd tossed and turned for nights as Meg's pending return drew closer. Bella's words kept running through her head: *"The six million dollar question is, do you love her?"*

If this scenario had played out three months ago, Allie's answer would have been an unequivocal yes, but with Meg's heart attack, it felt as if everything had changed.

She thought back across the years that she and Meg had known each other. The adventures, the near misses, the fun and laughter they had shared. The only time they had really been apart was after Allie had started her relationship with Julia. Much to Allie's distress, Meg and Julia had never gotten along. Three days after Julia announced she and Allie were moving in together, Meg came by to say she was leaving for Paris. Nothing Allie could say would change her mind, and two days later, Meg flew out of her life. Other than a few postcards and the occasional phone call, nearly two years went by without any contact from Meg at all.

Then just as suddenly as she had left, Meg was back, with Francoise, a tall, gorgeous French woman she'd met in Paris. They set up house several suburbs away from Allie and Julia. At first, Allie had just been thrilled to have Meg back in town, but she'd soon found herself resenting Francoise and what she perceived as her leaching off Meg's good nature. With Meg's return, Allie's relationship with Julia had begun to deteriorate, and six months later, Julia's resentment had finally boiled over.

———◦∞◦———

"All you want to do is spend time with Meg. Honestly, I don't know what you have to talk about. You don't do anything except cook at that stupid restaurant!" Julia accused her angrily one night.

That smarted. Allie's five-star Sydney restaurant was always convenient to drop into conversation when Julia was trying to impress a friend or colleague.

"Perhaps the fact that she appreciates me and my skills has something to do with it," Allie replied. "You've always been jealous of my friendship with Meg."

"I thought when we started going out together that I would have all of you. Unfortunately, I was wrong, because the bigger part of you has always belonged to Meg and that's never going to change."

Allie threw her hands in the air. "Again with this conversation. When are you going to let this go?"

Julia took a breath. "All right, let's do this, right here, right now."

Allie frowned, feeling her anger build. "Do what exactly?"

"I'm giving you an ultimatum. I want you to cut your ties with Meg totally. We can just go back to how it was before Meg came back from France. Can you do that?"

Allie stared at her in amazement. "Are you serious?"

"As far as I'm concerned, it's the only way this relationship can keep going. I'm sick and tired of playing second fiddle to another woman. If you love me enough, you'll give her up. Otherwise, it's not fair to ask me to stay."

Allie continued to stare at her in disbelief, then started to laugh. Suddenly, the whole situation seemed to have resolved itself with a clarity that surprised her.

Taken aback, Julia smiled. "Is that a yes?"

Allie shook her head, still bemused by Julia's suggestion. "No. I'm sorry, but I could no more give up Meg than I could give up breathing. She's my closest friend and has been for nearly twenty years and I don't give up my friends for anyone. The fact that you would even ask me shows that this relationship is even more doomed than I thought." She paused for a moment, studying Julia's surly expression. "I do, however, think you're right about one thing. It is unfair of me to ask you to stay, so please, feel free to leave whenever it is convenient."

When Julia packed her belongings and walked out two nights later, Allie realised the enormity of what she'd done. Her instinctive reaction was to ring Meg. Within the hour, Meg was on her doorstep, offering sympathy and a shoulder to cry on. For some reason, Allie was reluctant to tell Meg of Julia's accusations regarding their friendship, instead alluding to general jealousy as the reason for their breakup.

Within weeks, Meg and Allie easily fell back into their old routine and it was several months before Allie realised that Francoise was no longer around.

"She went back to Paris," Meg confessed when questioned.

"Why didn't you tell me? What happened?"

Meg shrugged. "It ran its course; it ended. No big deal."

Allie shook her head at the memory. That was so typical of Meg. She had an ability to just walk away from lovers when relationships ended, seemingly without a backwards glance. Allie, on the other hand, usually weighed up the pros and cons, discussed, agonised and changed her mind at least twenty times. Finally, in frustration, Meg would ask her the same question: "Do you love her?"

Thinking back on the relationships she'd had over the years, Allie could honestly say that while there were several women she had been seriously in lust with, there weren't any that she had truly loved. There was only one person in her life she had loved, one person she knew better than she knew herself and trusted with her life.

"Meg!" she whispered into the cool quiet of the deserted beer garden.

As she finally acknowledged the reality, Allie felt the last of her defences crumble. Now it was out in the open, Allie knew she had to take the biggest risk of her life.

Leaving her half-drunk wine, she walked back to her rented room, collected her bags, checked out and headed home.

Chapter 28

ALLIE HESITANTLY KNOCKED ON MEG'S front door, still unsure exactly what she was going to say. How do you tell someone you have known for decades that you love her without sounding like an idiot? What if Bella was wrong and Meg didn't love her the same way? She could be about to make a total fool of herself. What if...?

"Allie. You're back." Meg's shock at seeing Allie made her words sharper than she'd intended.

Allie stepped back, her dismay at Meg's tone clear on her face.

Meg shook her head in frustration, "I'm sorry, that came out wrong. Please, come in."

The two women stared at each other, neither seemingly able to move. Eventually, Meg broke the spell and stepped back to usher Allie inside. In the living room, Allie stood whilst Meg poured her a glass of wine.

"Should you be drinking?" Allie asked, frowning, indicating the half-empty glass by Meg's chair.

Meg shrugged. "I'm allowed to have one glass every couple of days, at least for the next couple of months."

"So, how are you?" asked Allie curtly, accepting the glass Meg handed her.

Meg studied her friend with concern. Allie had lost weight and looked gaunt and tired.

"Well I certainly feel better than you look," she responded with her usual honesty, taking a seat in her armchair.

Allie's pent up anger exploded. "Well that's bloody marvellous! That has probably got a lot to do with the fact that you've been in hospital for the last five weeks, having everyone running around after you, while the rest of us were worrying ourselves sick."

Meg started to speak and then stopped, at a loss. Finally she said, "I'm so sorry, Allie. I know I should have told you what was happening to me."

"Yes, you damn well should have!" Allie put the glass down on the table and glared at Meg. "You had no right to push me away. For heaven's sake, what did you think I was going to do? After all the enquiries I made and the conversations we had, how did you not understand that I was concerned about you? I knew there was something wrong, Meg. Why the hell wouldn't you talk to me?"

Meg sat with her head bowed, cradling her wine, speechless.

"I thought you were going to die, Meg. When I saw you on that gurney before they took you to hospital, I thought I'd lost you and I was bloody terrified. Have you any idea what that feels like?" Allie turned away, walking towards the window as tears threatened to choke her. "And then..." She gave a mocking laugh. "Oh, then I found out that the whole thing could have been prevented, if you'd told someone what you were experiencing. Imagine, if you can, how that made me feel?" Lowering her voice, she spoke through gritted teeth, "Right there and then, I was so furious with you, I almost wished you had died."

Meg blanched. Allie's words hung in the air. She had seen Allie angry in the past, but never this angry and never, ever had the anger been directed towards her.

"For weeks, wherever I went, people were asking me for details about your heart attack, as if I might actually know something." Allie leant her head against the cool window and clenched her fists. "I desperately wanted to hate you. You have no idea how bloody hard I tried," Allie choked.

She heard a small sob and turned to look at Meg, shocked to see tears running down her face. Instantly, her anger evaporated. Slumping onto the sofa, she dropped her head into her hands, then looked across at Meg's tear-stained face and gave a small smile.

"No matter how hard I tried, though, I just couldn't hate you. Do you know how hard it is to hate someone you are in love with?" she asked quietly.

Meg wiped her cheeks, dabbed at her eyes and returned Allie's gaze. Emotion vibrated around them, like an electrical current bridging the gap between them. Meg rose from her chair, holding Allie's gaze as she walked the few feet to the sofa, then sat next to her. Taking Allie's hands, she held them close to her chest.

"I am so sorry, my darling. You're right. I was being stupid and selfish and not thinking about you at all. I was thinking about me, and the fact that I wanted to be strong and not give in to weakness. I am so, so sorry that I caused you so much pain."

Allie sighed and squeezed Meg's hand. "Oh, for heaven's sake, when are you going to learn that you aren't bloody superwoman?" Exhaustion crept into her voice as she continued, "I honestly don't know what I would have done if I had lost you. I don't know how I would have ever kept going." Letting go of Meg's hand, Allie gave a small shrug. "Knowing that, I actually don't know if I can just continue the way we were. I really don't."

Taking a deep breath, Allie chose her next words carefully, praying she was making the right decision. "I have spent a lot of time thinking about our history and I realise that, whilst what you did was incredibly stupid, you are not the only one at fault here." Lifting Meg's chin with her hand, she looked directly into her eyes. "I'm in love with you, Meg. I have always been in love with you, but I have never been confident enough to acknowledge it to myself, let alone to you. What I need to know now is, do you love me?"

Meg's eyes widened, a flash of fierceness lighting up her expression. She leant over and took Allie's face in her hands, drawing her lips to her as she whispered, "More than anyone in the world."

How did I not know that Meg's lips would be so soft? Allie wondered as she surrendered to the demanding mouth moving against hers. She felt like Alice in Wonderland, falling, falling, falling through the rabbit hole. All she was aware of was Meg's voice softly saying her name over and over again, like a prayer, as she spilled kisses over her cheeks and down her neck. This was what she had been missing all those years; holding Meg like this felt like coming home. She lifted her head, stroking Meg's face, and the desire radiating from her left Allie breathless.

Together they moved to the bedroom, slowly, taking their time, pausing to seek one another's lips time and again.

They were soon standing beside Meg's bed, whispering endearments, encouraging, wanting, hands and lips moving in synchronicity. Allie felt Meg's hesitation as she began to remove her shirt.

"The operation, I have to be careful..." she began.

Seeing the fear in Meg's eyes, Allie paused, laying a finger against Meg's lips. "Trust me, my darling."

Meg smiled slowly, gently stroking Allie's cheek. "I do. I trust you more than anyone in the world. I always have."

As the shadows of the encroaching evening crept over the comforter covering the two women, Allie stirred in Meg's arms.

"Why didn't you ever tell me how you felt?" she asked quietly.

Tracing her fingers over the back of Allie's hand, Meg shook her head. "Oh, you have no idea how many times I tried, but I never quite knew how. We had settled into such a comfortable space with one another. I nearly summoned up the courage several times, but then failed at the last minute. I was terrified you'd reject me and then I would lose it all; you and our friendship. As the years went on, it just seemed easier to ignore my feelings. Then one day, I talked myself into taking the risk. It was the week of your thirty-fifth birthday. I had spent days practising what I was going to say to you and even had a romantic surprise dinner booked. I told myself that if you said no, it would be all right, we would still be friends. I rang to invite you to dinner..."

Allie closed her eyes, groaning as she remembered. "And I told you that I couldn't because I was going to dinner with this wonderful new woman I'd met. Oh, Meg..."

Meg shrugged. "I told myself it was a small setback. You hadn't been in a real relationship for several years. I figured it would last a few weeks, as usual, and then I could try again. Imagine my complete shock when you announced several months later that the two of you were moving in together."

Allie's eyes widened and she sat up, staring at Meg intently. "That's why you suddenly took off to France."

"I never liked that bloody woman anyway, but it was so hard to be around you and see you so happy. I know, it sounds strange, but I loved you so much it hurt. I tried for a while, but when it became obvious that she was using you and you refused to listen to me, I got incredibly angry and decided to get as far away as possible. I had this crazy notion that you would come to your senses and come after me." Meg rolled her eyes. "When you didn't, well...I guess I decided that it was just all a pipe dream."

Allie linked her fingers through Meg's. "You came back, though, in the end," she said softly, nestling once more in Meg's arms.

Meg smiled sadly. "Yes, my darling, but I came back with a protective shield around my heart. I couldn't bear being away from you any longer, so I decided I just had to hide my feelings. I thought I was doing fairly well, but apparently there are others around who aren't so easily fooled."

"I can't believe we have both been such fools for so long! You know, for two smart women, we have been pretty damned stupid."

Meg drew Allie closer. "Maybe, but I tend to think that things work out the way they're meant to. Whatever the past is, we can't change it. We can only go forward."

"Well," said Allie, running her hands over Meg's body, "at least we will be doing that together."

Chapter 29

UPON RETURNING FROM THEIR EARLY morning walk, Sparrow and Daphne decided to call in on Meg to see if she wanted to join them for dinner that evening. They hadn't had a chance to catch up with her since she had been released from hospital and they wanted to make sure she was settling back in comfortably. Just as they reached Meg's cottage, Sparrow stopped.

"Allie's back," she noted, indicating the small, blue hatchback parked in the opposite driveway.

"Well, she had to come back sooner or later," Daphne replied. "I mean, it's not as if she could stay away forever. I still say there is a lot more going on with those two than they'll admit, though what they're waiting for is beyond me."

"Well, honey, they just have to work it out themselves. All we can do is be here and support them. If they decide to just be friends, there's not much we can do about it."

"Well, I hope now that Meg is back, they sort out their problems. I would hate to see the potential for such a strong relationship not work out."

Daphne knocked on Meg's door. When there was no response, Sparrow checked her watch.

"Maybe it's too early. I mean, it is only eight-fifteen on a Sunday morning. Maybe we should go and come back a bit later?"

Daphne chewed her lip. "Well, as long as she's not in trouble. But what if something has happened to her and she has had another attack? I'm knocking again."

Daphne knocked more forcibly, calling out Meg's name as she did so. Finally, the door opened to reveal a somewhat dishevelled Meg glaring at them.

"You two do know it is eight-fifteen on Sunday morning, don't you? I hope whatever it is that has you knocking on my door at this ungodly hour is urgent." Meg sounded cross as she tightened the belt on her robe.

Sparrow, who had never seen Meg anything but beautifully dressed, smiled at the apparition in the doorway.

"Sorry, Meg." Daphne shuffled her feet and looked across at Sparrow. "We just wanted to make sure you were all right."

Meg raised an eyebrow, then chuckled at her visitors. "So, you came by at eight-fifteen to wake me up and check on me?"

Putting her hand on Daphne's arm, Sparrow laughed. "Well, we also came to invite you to dinner tonight, but if you can't make it that's…"

"Darling, where are you? Coffee's ready; do you want it in bed?"

Daphne and Sparrow stood rooted to the spot as Allie appeared, dressed only in a large blue button down shirt and looking every bit as dishevelled as Meg.

"Oh, hello you two," Allie said in surprise, drawing up next to Meg.

Daphne's face was crimson with embarrassment as she stammered, "Hi, Allie. Sorry to interrupt. We, uh…um…"

Sparrow recovered faster. "Yes," she said, taking Daphne's arm and firmly leading her away. "We will let you get on with… I mean, we'll talk to you both later."

Meg and Allie watched the two hurriedly make their escape. Closing the front door, they both leant against it, laughing helplessly.

Wiping tears from her eyes, Meg shook her head. "You should have seen the expression on Daphne's face when she heard your voice. I thought she was going to swallow her tongue," she gasped.

Allie chuckled. "Well I really don't think they expected this scenario when they came knocking on your door. Thank heavens Sparrow was with Daphne, or she would probably still be standing outside with that deer in the headlights expression on her face."

Still chuckling, they moved to the kitchen.

"Before we were so rudely interrupted, we were going to have breakfast. Are you still hungry?" Meg asked with a silly grin and a raised eyebrow.

Allie untied the belt on Meg's robe. "Totally ravenous, and I know just what will settle my hunger."

⋯⟡⋯

Allie stood in Meg's warm sunlit kitchen, busily preparing breakfast. Humming softly as she mixed the ingredients for a Spanish omelette in a bowl, she glanced over at Meg reading the paper.

"I guess we have been well and truly sprung," she commented, heating up the pan and adding the contents of the bowl. "Word is going to get around the community pretty quickly."

Meg peered at her over the top of her reading glasses. "Do you mind?"

Allie hesitated, then, seeing Meg's open expression turn to hurt, she rushed to explain. "No darling, of course I don't. I guess if I'd had a choice, I would have just liked to have kept it to ourselves a little longer. You know, be in control of who, what and when we told. There's no way this story is going to be kept quiet. I have the feeling that a number of people will be having a joke at our expense."

Giving an appreciative sniff, Meg shrugged. "That's people, honey. We'll be a story for a few weeks and then they'll settle down. The people that know and love us will be delighted; the rest, well, they'll just busy themselves with gossip."

Allie lowered the heat and poured in the egg. She couldn't remember the number of times she had stood just like this, making breakfast for them both while Meg shared snippets of news from the paper. Allie wondered again how she could not have realised that what they shared was so much more than just a deep friendship. She was still in a daze over the power of the sexual rush they were sharing. Who knew she could still feel like a teenager in lust? As she glanced across at Meg, she felt happiness suffuse every fibre of her body.

"If you keep looking at me with that goofy look on your face, you'll burn that omelette," Meg warned without looking up from the paper.

Allie walked over and wrapped her arms around her. "Never burnt one yet, don't intend to start now."

She nibbled Meg's ear and Meg put the paper down and turned to face her. Taking Allie's hands in hers, Meg sighed and gently pulled her onto her lap. Leaning her forehead against Allie's, she asked quietly, "Are you happy? Is this what you really want? Because if it's not, you have to tell me now."

Hearing the whisper of anxiety in Meg's voice, Allie held her close. "Yes, it is what I want and I couldn't be happier." Taking her lover's face in her hands, she ran her thumbs tenderly along her cheekbones. "I love you, Meg. It might have taken me over forty years to acknowledge it, but now I've seen the light, you're well and truly stuck with me. I have no idea what our future holds but as long we are sharing it, I don't care."

Meg smiled, giving her a gentle kiss. "Well then, woman, you'd better feed me, because I see a certain amount of activity that is going to take a fair bit of energy in the very near future."

Chapter 30

SUMMER

CARO LOUNGED BACK ON THE sofa watching Louise iron her shirts. Clad in nothing but cut off shorts and a sleeveless T-shirt, Louise's lean, tan body was far more interesting to watch than the television show playing out in front of her. She was finding the smell of freshly ironed cotton and the whisper of the iron against the shirt surprisingly erotic. A prickle of desire spread through her as Louise bent to examine a wrinkle and her shirt rode up slightly, exposing an expanse of tanned, bare skin that Caro longed to run her tongue along.

Watching the muscles in Louise's arm flex as she pushed the iron across the garment, Caro remembered how strong those arms felt around her. As Louise placed the freshly ironed shirt on a hanger, Caro noticed the now damp T-shirt clinging to her breasts and a tendril of loose hair laying carelessly across her cheek.

Louise bent low to pick another garment from the ironing basket, her well-toned backside straining against her shorts, and Caro felt her breath quickening, surprised that she had never realised that ironing could be such an incredibly erotic activity. Lost in a haze of domestic lust, she suddenly realised that Louise had stopped ironing and was instead looking at her with a questioning grin.

"Um, sorry, what did you say?" she asked, trying to collect herself.

"I said, if you don't stop looking at me like that, we are both going to burst into flames."

Caro smiled at her through half-closed eyes. "Well," she said huskily, "you do create a certain type of picture in my mind."

Turning the iron off, Louise made her way slowly towards her. "Oh, yes?" she whispered, slowly positioning herself over Caro, who was lying back on the couch. "And what kind of a picture would that be exactly?"

Caro reached for her, ran her hands along Louise's back. She licked a single bead of sweat that was rolling down Louise's neck, and felt her nipples harden behind the damp shirt.

"An incredibly sexy one," she purred. "I think you should give up your day job and just stay home and iron."

Louise raised an eyebrow. "I think both of us know that's never going to happen. However," she moved her hips slowly against her lover, "if you ask me nicely, I am sure I can be persuaded to iron when the need arises."

Rolling Louise onto the couch next to her, Caro traced her fingers over her abdomen then slowly into her shorts, running her fingers through the mound of short hair. Feeling Louise's immediate response to her explorations, she teased with light strokes, marvelling at her rapidly changing breathing pattern. Louise's lips finally claimed her, her tongue urging Caro to explore deeper, searching for release.

"Talking of need arising," Louise growled, breaking the kiss, feeling Caro's excitement rising to match her own.

Caro's strokes became harder and faster, their bodies matching each other in a sensual synchronicity that was as natural as breathing. Feeling the pressure mounting, Caro kissed Louise hard as both women tumbled into an orgasm that left them limp and gasping, holding each other so closely it felt as though their skin was merging.

Caro could feel Louise's heart pounding against her own chest and felt contentment wash over her. There were times when they were both so busy that they barely saw each other from one end of the day to the next. She was so grateful that, despite their demanding schedules, their connection always grounded them. No matter what chaos surrounded them, a simple look or touch could immediately bring them back to each other.

Louise stirred in Caro's arms. "I love you," she murmured sleepily.

Caro kissed her gently. "I love you too, honey. Always have, always will."

Finally, Louise sat up, stretched, then rested her arms across Caro's shoulders, holding her close. "You know, I realised again the other day when I was going through the photographic and video presentation, that I couldn't have created OWL's Haven if you hadn't come back home from America when I asked you to."

Caro ran her fingers through Louise's hair. "We were always a good pair. Even before I left I knew that. I think we both needed to spread our wings. My years working in the States allowed for that."

Louise smiled, remembering her call to Caro, after years apart, asking her to come home to help oversee the construction of OWL's Haven. She trusted Caro more than anyone and knew she was the one person who could manage such an important and ambitious project.

"I still remember you in muddy work boots, giving hell to tardy builders and inefficient council inspectors. Watching you working your magic was what made me realise I had never stopped loving you. I had just buried it for a while."

Caro smiled. "Well, it took time, but I'm so glad you made that phone call. I realised, too, that I was still in love with you. Still am." Caro leant in for a gentle kiss. "I think we can now agree that if we could survive the drama of creating OWL's Haven, then we can survive anything."

Louise stretched again, causing her T-shirt shirt to ride up further and expose her taut abdomen. Caro's expression grew lustful, and Louise laughed.

"Oh, don't even think about it. I need a shower, a cup of coffee and food, in that order."

Caro pretended to pout. "Spoil sport."

Louise pulled her up for a quick kiss on the lips. "I didn't say no. I just said not now. Let's get cleaned up, refuelled and see where the night takes us."

Chapter 31

MEG WOKE TO THE SOUNDS of cheering outside her bedroom window. Unable to decipher what the noise was, she sat up, inadvertently moving the sheet and revealing Allie's naked body. A rush of emotions swirled through her as she watched her lover sleeping. Love, tenderness, lust. *Oh, my heaven*, she thought. Lust like she had never experienced. Meg had never been shy about sex; she'd had lovers all over the world, but none had ever touched her heart. When the time had come for her to move on, she had always been able to walk away with no regrets. The passion that she and Allie had shared over the past weeks, though, had been building over a lifetime, and the knowledge that they would continue to build on this love filled her with extraordinary joy.

As if aware of Meg's scrutiny, Allie stretched and opened her eyes. Hearing the renewed round of cheering, her eyes widened as she and Meg looked at each other in surprise.

"The vote!" they both exclaimed at the same time.

"Damn, where's the bloody remote?" Meg swore, looking around. As Allie swept back the coverlet, the elusive control fell to the floor, where Meg scrambled for it.

On the television, they were greeted by the scene of thousands of rainbow covered supporters gathered outside

Parliament House in Canberra. The ticker tape running along the bottom of the screen announced the news that the Australian government had passed the Same Sex Marriage Bill.

"Oh my God!" Allie shouted in wonder.

"They've damn well gone and passed it," Meg added in disbelief.

Hugging each other, the two women sat up in bed and watched the details unfold on the screen.

Suddenly there was the sound of banging on Meg's front door.

"Hey, you two love birds, get out here. There's a party happening," a voice called.

Quickly putting on a robe, Meg stuck her head out the window to see Pat, Daphne, Bella and several other women outside her cottage, all with glasses of champagne in their hands.

"We'll be right out, just give us a minute," she called.

"Don't make us come in and get you," warned Pat with a laugh.

Twenty minutes later, Meg and Allie joined the growing group partying outside on the street. Everyone was laughing as the realisation that the vote had finally been won began to hit home.

"So what happened to you two?" Daphne asked with feigned innocence, handing them each a glass of champagne. "I thought you were coming to watch the vote with us. Did you get a better offer?"

Sparrow poked Daphne in the arm. "Stop teasing them. You've made Allie blush."

Allie smiled and took a sip of champagne. "Meg was tired and I thought it would be better for her to lie down, and then I thought I'd lie down too, just to keep her company. Suddenly, we realised we weren't quite as tired as we thought. Besides, Casey was apparently insistent that Meg get enough exercise, so I decided I would do whatever I could to make sure she followed those instructions. What's a woman to do?" Allie asked, shrugging innocently.

"Whoa, too much information," cried Daphne, putting her hands over her ears, while the other women roared with laughter.

"Teach you to try and embarrass her," Meg smugly retorted.

Catching sight of Leslie's T-shirt, Daphne stared incredulously. "Where on earth did you find that?"

Leslie proudly turned so they could all read the motif emblazoned across the front: 'So dip me in honey and throw me to the lesbians'.'

"Why do you ask, Daphne? Do you have a sweet tooth?" Leslie asked with a wink.

"I'm pleading diabetes," Daphne replied, throwing up her hands and laughing.

As the group continued to tease Leslie, Daphne turned to Pat. "So, now that it's legal, are you going to marry Bella?"

Pat watched Bella chatting to one of the other residents. "If she'll have me," she declared simply. "What about you and Sparrow?"

Daphne frowned. "Well, it's early days yet, but I'm not really the marrying kind. I mean, I don't need to marry her to prove how much I love her. What we have is between ourselves. However, just because I don't choose to marry, doesn't mean I still shouldn't have the right to if I want to."

As the crowd grew, the partying moved to the clubhouse, until one by one, the residents called it a night. Waving goodnight to Pat and Bella, Allie and Meg returned home.

"Well that was some celebration," Meg declared with a yawn, shedding her clothes and falling into bed.

"I know. I'm so tired I can barely think. I don't remember when I last danced so much. I think I might have put my back out." Allie winced.

As Meg watched Allie undress and climb naked into bed, tiredness battled with her libido. "If I were twenty years younger..." she murmured sleepily.

Turning off the bedside lamp, Allie gathered Meg into her arms, kissing her forehead.

"I bet you say that to all the girls," she whispered.

Chapter 32

BELLA WAS WORKING ON A watercolour painting outside in their pergola when Pat came home from her walk.

"Look who I found outside our front door," she announced.

Hearing the uncertainty in her voice, Bella turned quickly to see Pat standing with Jenny Wilcox. Bella saw the sudden fear that she felt reflected in her lover's eyes. They had been waiting for the final results of Bella's follow up tests, the results that would tell her whether or not she had beaten the cancer. The last seven months had been a roller coaster ride for them both, and they desperately wanted to believe it had been successful, as the alternative was something neither wanted to contemplate.

Putting her paintbrush down and moving away from her easel, Bella motioned for Jenny to sit down. Pat quickly moved to stand by Bella.

"I wanted to come and see you both in person." Jenny smiled. "I always believe that giving good news is the best possible way to start the day. I have to say that yours is the best news I can possibly give." She took a deep breath. "Bella, your results are in and all indications are that the tumour has gone."

Bella stood and threw her arms around Pat. The two women held one another as their tears flowed. Eventually, Bella released her hold on Pat and turned to Jenny. Opening her arms, she indicated for her to join them. The three women embraced, silently acknowledging their shared joy and relief.

"Thank you," Bella whispered through her tears. "Thank you for looking after me so well, for everything you did for both of us while I was sick. I was so lucky to have you as my doctor."

"Bella's right, we couldn't have done this without you," Pat added huskily.

Jenny laughed, wiping her eyes. "No, Bella, the determination that you showed, and the support that Pat gave you while you were fighting this damned awful disease, is what beat this. You're two remarkable women and I'm just so incredibly happy that it's ended so well."

Still stunned, Bella sat down, pulling Pat onto the seat next to her. "So what's next? Do I still need to continue having regular tests?"

"Well, in light of your past history, it would be advisable to have a check-up every six months. I'll make sure I schedule that into my diary, but for now, just go and enjoy life. I see lots of celebration in your future," Jenny said, laughing as she picked up her bag and made her way to the front door. "Are you happy to tell Louise and Caro, or would you like me to do it?"

"Would you mind if we did it? It'll be a wonderful chance for us to thank them for all they have done for us as well. We have so many people to thank and so many reasons to be grateful," Bella replied as she opened the door.

Waving goodbye to Jenny, Bella closed the door, then wrapped Pat in her arms. They stood holding each other, sobbing, finally able to let go. After several minutes, Pat gently kissed the top of Bella's head.

"I can't believe it's over," Bella said, looking up at Pat. "The longer we had to wait, the more worried I became. Although I hoped with all my heart for a second chance, I knew the odds weren't good. It feels like we've been given a new life."

"Yes, I guess in a way we have," Pat agreed softly, wiping Bella's tears.

"You have a new me."

"Nah, I'll take the old one. She was always the woman for me," Pat murmured, continuing to stroke Bella's face. "In fact, now it's legal, I would like to officially keep you for the rest of our lives."

Bella smiled at Pat. "*Cara*, of course... Oh." She stopped as the meaning of Pat's words sank in. "Do you mean you... you want to marry me?"

"I've wanted to marry you from the first moment I saw you." Taking both of Bella's hands in hers, Pat carefully lowered herself down to one knee. "Bella Patricia Fiorisi, will you do me the incredible honour of marrying me, becoming my wife and making me possibly the happiest woman on earth?"

"Oh, Pat, of course I'll marry you!" Bella laughed through her tears. Her attempt to help her lover stand resulted in Bella ending unceremoniously on the floor and both women dissolving into peals of joyful laughter.

"Oh, good Lord, we may have to call someone to help us up," Bella gasped when she was finally able to speak.

"Or we could take advantage of the situation and stay right where we are," Pat suggested, sliding her fingers inside Bella's blouse.

Bella's answering kiss was the only reply Pat needed.

Chapter 33

MEG AND ALLIE WALKED UP the flagstone front steps of Gabby's, Berry's premiere four-star restaurant, lit up in all its evening glory. Allie again admired the gracious old homestead in which the restaurant was housed. Jasmine and wisteria vines graced the wide veranda, and through the open windows came the soft sounds of music and laughter.

"This is such a gorgeous venue," Allie sighed, taking Meg's arm as they walked inside. "I just love coming here."

"It also helps that it's one of the only restaurants that serves meals as marvellous as yours," Meg replied, squeezing Allie's arm.

Meg and Allie were greeted warmly by the staff, who directed them to one of the elegant private dining rooms. Taking glasses of champagne as they entered, they made their way over to a small cluster of women standing by the open windows.

"Good evening, everyone," Allie greeted Sparrow, Daphne, Louise and Caro. "What are you discussing so intently?"

"Hello, you two," Caro smiled. "We are just wondering if anyone has any idea of why Pat and Bella have invited us all to dinner?"

"Meg and I just got the invitation the other day. Pat called in and apologised for the short notice, but stressed that it was really important that we turn up. Apart from that, she refused to say anything." Allie scanned the room. "Judging by the number of residents here, though, whatever the reason, it must be big."

"Well, an opportunity to come to this wonderful restaurant with our friends was too good for us to turn down," Sparrow declared excitedly. "It is such a treat to see everyone dressed up."

"I had to try and find something decent to wear," laughed Daphne. "The only things I seem to have these days are shorts, jeans and cargo pants."

"Well, there is certainly lots of colour and movement here tonight and everyone looks very elegant," Louise remarked.

"Allie!" Turning at the sound of her name, Allie found herself enveloped in a hug from Pat. "Thank you all so much for coming."

Allie laughed. "A surprise invitation to our favourite restaurant with all our friends? How on earth could we possibly say no to that? It's what you call a lay down…damn, what's the word?" she asked, turning to Meg.

"*Misere*." Meg smiled.

"Yes, that's it. Anyway," she indicated their group, "we're also extremely curious as to why we are all here."

Pat laughed. "Everything will be revealed in time, you just have to be patient."

A gentle gong interrupted the conversation.

Pat turned. "I believe that is the request for everyone to take their seats so that dinner can be served. Enjoy yourselves, and Bella and I will catch up with you later."

Watching Pat walk away, Allie turned to the others. "Well, I guess we are just going to have to wait and see."

"So, I believe that you and Meg have moved in together?" Daphne asked as their main course plates were being cleared.

Allie beamed. "Yes, a couple of weeks ago."

"It seemed ridiculous for us to have separate houses, so we decided that since my place is bigger, Allie should move in with me," Meg said gently, laying her hand on Allie's. "I'm still getting used to believing that we have the rest of our lives together."

"Well, cheers to you both," Caro said, raising her glass. "It might have taken a while, but in the end, love won out!"

Acknowledging the toast, Meg fixed Daphne and Sparrow with a piercing stare and asked innocently, "So, when are you two moving in together?"

Daphne coloured, looking at Sparrow. "Oh...well..."

The sound of a tinkling bell interrupted their conversation and drew their attention to the centre table, where Bella was seated with Pat standing behind, her hands on Bella's shoulders.

As the hubbub died away, Pat cleared her throat, looking with affection at the faces of their many friends.

"Firstly, Bella and I would like to welcome you all here tonight and thank you so much for coming. I know you are all curious as to the reason for tonight's party, though knowing this group, most of you don't need any excuse for a party." Pat smiled as laughter bubbled through the room.

"When Bella and I arrived at OWL's Haven, eight years ago, we knew very few lesbians. We had spent much of our life together hidden away, living quietly and trying not to attract attention to ourselves. Coming here was the most wonderful experience for both of us. From being two of very few, we became two of many. We have made friendships that I hope will last us the rest of our lives and we have enjoyed so many wonderful times. When Bella became sick, there were so many people who offered support, not just for Bella, but also for me." Looking down at her partner, she smiled. "I know Bella joins me in saying that without everyone here, we would not have been able to get through those horrible dark days...which brings me to the first reason for this celebration dinner."

Bella leant her head back slightly to rest it against Pat's chest, her eyes shimmering with tears as she gazed around the room.

"Dr Wilcox confirmed for us earlier this week that the final results of Bella's tests have come through." Taking a deep breath, Pat placed a gentle kiss on Bella's head. "The tests came back negative. Bella is in the clear."

For a brief moment no-one moved, then suddenly the room erupted.

"She made it," Allie gasped, wiping her tears. "I knew she'd make it; she's such a fighter."

Thrilled, she joined everyone else as they stood, clapping and cheering in celebration. Several made their way to the couple, congratulating them with hugs and kisses. Allie grabbed Meg, both of them laughing with sheer relief and joy.

After a few moments, a beaming Pat called the room to order. "There is one more thing that we would like to share with you all. You would think that Bella having a clean bill of health would be enough to make me the happiest woman alive, but there is one more thing that has made me happier than I could ever imagine."

Pat grinned at the puzzled anticipation of her audience. Catching Daphne's eye, she saw her answering smile of encouragement.

"Bella has also agreed to be my wife, and we would like to take this opportunity to invite you all to our wedding."

Once again, the room erupted in cheers. Both women were again swamped with hugs and kisses.

Daphne pulled Pat into a huge hug. "You finally did it," she exclaimed joyfully. "It's only taken you about forty years."

"Well, you know how it is," Pat laughed. "I wouldn't want to rush anything."

Allie took Bella's hand. "I can't tell you how delighted I am for you, for both of you."

Bella beamed, squeezing Allie's hand tight. "I am so incredibly happy. How did I get so lucky?"

Meg leant in to give Bella a kiss on the cheek. "You deserve every minute of happiness, but are you sure you want us old reprobates at the wedding? You know what some people are like when they have had a few drinks." She winked at Allie.

"You are not getting out of it that easily, Meg," Pat said, giving her a kiss on the cheek. "We are having a wedding, and you are coming."

"Have you set a date yet?" Sparrow asked.

"Yes, the twenty-eighth of March." Pat looked down at Bella, holding her gaze, as Bella continued, "It's the anniversary of when we first met."

"Our first wedding at OWL's Haven," crowed Louise. "What a wonderful start to the year."

"Well, there isn't much time. We need to start the wedding planning right away," cautioned Allie.

While the women around her discussed wedding details, Pat watched Bella surrounded by their friends. An overwhelming feeling of love and contentment flowed through her, taking her breath away. As if sensing her thoughts, Bella turned towards her and Pat could see the answering love radiating in her eyes. Whatever had gone before, Pat knew that their future was going to be wonderful.

Chapter 34

MEG AND ALLIE SAT AT an outdoor table with Leslie and her friend Jenna, watching over the passing parade of visitors as they wandered through the grounds. The OWL's Haven Ten Year Anniversary Party was off to a tremendous start and visitors were everywhere, stopping to admire the gardens or to greet one another in boisterous groups.

"What a wonderful turnout," Jenna gushed.

Allie looked around. All possible vantage points were festooned with rainbow banners, balloons and streamers, and the sound of music from a string quartet floated across the gardens.

"It is pretty spectacular, isn't it?" Allie confirmed. "It seems to have been coming for such a long time and now it's here, I have to confess, I am quite excited."

"Well, when you look around, you can see why it took so long to organise," Meg said.

Allie agreed. "They seem to have thought of everything. Entertainment, music, quiet spaces..."

"...and thankfully, lots of places to sit," interrupted Meg, leaning back in her chair.

"So what's the line-up for the day?" Leslie asked.

Allie read from the elegant program in her hands. "Well it says here that there will be the formal welcome at twelve thirty, at one p.m. lunch will be served in the main marquee and at two thirty the choirs will start their performances."

"Well, at least they are serving drinks and snacks before lunch. If I had to wait until one p.m. before I could eat anything I might fade away," Leslie grumbled.

Meg watched Leslie pick at a plate piled high with a selection of delicious morsels, two glasses of champagne lined up alongside her plate.

"In actual fact, they aren't snacks, they're canapés," she corrected crisply. "And you aren't supposed to eat them by the plateful. You are only meant to have a couple; they're an appetiser, you heathen."

"My mother always used to call them finger food," Jenna interjected, nibbling on a tiny quiche.

Leslie guffawed. "They sure don't taste anything like the finger food I am used to eating."

As Meg huffed and rolled her eyes, Allie shook her head. Meg rose to the bait every time.

Spying Daphne and Sparrow, Allie called them over. "Where have you two been?" she asked as they arrived at the table.

"We have just been to see the exhibition of the history of OWL's Haven," Sparrow said excitedly, taking a seat next to Allie. "It's amazing. There are photos from the first time that Louise saw this place. You wouldn't believe what it was like, just this huge neglected space surrounding the old house."

Accepting a glass of champagne from Meg, Daphne took a seat next to Sparrow. "They've kept it all," she added. "There's the original contract for purchase of the land, the architectural drawings and all the photos documenting almost every part of the building project, as well as newspaper articles and interviews. There's even a short film clip of the first open day. It's absolutely fascinating."

"There's a lovely photo of all the residents taken a month after OWL's opened," Sparrow interjected. "They all look so incredibly happy."

"Well, it was quite something wasn't it? It took them nearly five years from the start of the project until the doors opened. They had all kinds of setbacks; makes you wonder how they had the money to keep going," Allie commented, getting caught up in their enthusiasm.

Meg leant in to the group and confided quietly, "She won it."

A short silence followed. "What do you mean? Who won what?" Jenna asked.

Intrigued, the women huddled closer towards Meg, not wanting to miss a word.

"Louise," she replied. "My sources tell me that she won twenty million dollars in a New Year's Eve Lottery."

"Holy hell, are you serious?" Leslie asked.

Meg nodded. "Yes, and apparently this project had been her dream since she was a young woman. She and Caro had broken up several years earlier when Caro moved to New York for work. When Louise won the money, she rang her and asked her to come back home to help her create her dream. So, Caro came back, they rekindled their relationship, built OWL's and here we are today."

Jenna sat back in her seat. "Oh, what a beautiful story. I've often wondered how long those two have been together."

"Well, they met some serious challenges," Meg continued. "Apparently they fought the local council for nearly a year because one of the councillors was a total homophobe. He was all in favour of the village going ahead until it was explained to him that OWL's stood for Older Wiser Lesbians." Meg smirked as she related the story. "He nearly had a fit of apoplexy. The thought of having a complex with over one hundred lesbians in it was apparently more than he could cope with and the council put every blockade in the way. It apparently cost Louise a fortune in legal fees. What was worse, though, was the number of our community who declined to help them get OWL's started."

Sparrow frowned. "Why? Surely they could see how viable it was."

Meg shrugged. "Apparently not. I think it was jealousy. You know, there are still members of our community out there waiting for it to fail." Shaking her head, she took a sip of champagne. "Still, despite all the setbacks, they eventually got the support they needed and together they got it up and running. Even with all that money, it had to have been a huge amount of work."

"Well, I'll tell you what, they were both pretty stunning fifteen years ago. There is a photo of Caro in jeans and work boots on the site that caused me to take a second look," Daphne said with a twinkle in her eye.

Sparrow eyed her lover speculatively and raised her eyebrow. "Is that right, dear?"

The women laughed as Daphne blushed. "Well, I mean… it was just…"

Chuckling quietly, Sparrow kissed her. "You are so easy to tease," she murmured.

"Oooohhh," exclaimed Meg, sitting up quickly to look across the lawn. "Isn't that Amy Tang?"

As a senior government member and out lesbian, Amy's unwavering support had been paramount in the passing of the recent Same Sex Marriage Bill. Her partner and daughter joined her where she sat talking to a group of OWL's residents.

"Oh, and there's Annabelle Winchester and her husband Jonathon," Leslie said, pointing out a well-known actress.

Meg snorted. "Husband, phooey. Beard is a more appropriate title."

The women all turned to look questioningly at Meg, who sat calmly drinking her champagne.

Jenna glanced from Meg to the actress and back again. "What are you saying?" she asked incredulously.

Meg just raised an eyebrow and shrugged. "Well, all I'm saying is that anyone who was as much into women as she was when I knew her in the eighties couldn't possibly be straight. She was always closeted, so I expect she still is. Besides, it's common knowledge that Jonathon is as queer as we are."

The women watched Annabelle sign autographs for several guests. Turning to smile at the audience that had gathered around her, she caught sight of Meg, who gave her a small wave. Looking puzzled, Annabelle started to wave back. The women watched, fascinated, as a look of shock slowly crossed her face. Making sudden apologies to her fans, she grabbed a confused Jonathon and marched rapidly away from their table towards the main marquee.

Meg laughed. "Poor Annabelle. Obviously nothing has changed."

"But if she is that deep in the closet, why the hell would she come here today?" Sparrow asked.

Meg shrugged. "Probably because she is incredibly lonely and wants to be around other lesbians. She just can't admit it."

Jenna refilled their glasses from one of the bottles of champagne that Leslie had managed to pilfer from the refreshment marquee. "That's so sad. I mean it's not as if anyone would care. There are lots of actresses coming out. If Magda can do it, anyone can."

"Well, I guess she was from a different era. Most of her fans are in their seventies now. Maybe they wouldn't be so open minded."

As a sound check interrupted their conversation, the women looked across at the stage. Louise, Caro and several others were talking to a young man with a video camera near the microphones.

"Hello, I think the formalities might be about to start," Meg announced.

Sure enough, the small group, led by Caro, stepped up to the podium. Tapping the microphone, Louise waited until she had everyone's attention.

"Minister, Chair of the Board, board members, residents, ladies and gentlemen. I would like to welcome all of you here today for the tenth anniversary of the opening of OWL's Haven. I am not going to make a long speech, but I would like to acknowledge the enormous support of the board of directors. Without their belief in me and the continued support of all of our friends and benefactors, OWL's Haven would still only be the dream I had as a young woman."

Louise looked carefully at the women seated at the scattered tables around the front of the stage.

"To our amazing residents, I say thank you. Thank you for making OWL's Haven the place it is today. Without you, it would just be bricks and mortar and not the vibrant, wonderful community that we all love." As the loud cheering erupted, Louise smiled, waiting for the hubbub to quiet.

"We are all incredibly lucky to be supported by the best staff I could ever wish for. The assistance you give to me and the residents, the dedication, love and commitment you bring to your work, is valued far more than you will ever know."

Louise paused and turned to Caro. Reaching for her hand, she brought Caro to her side. "Finally, to my incredible partner Caro. Without your belief in OWL's Haven, this would never have been a possibility. You support me, love me, nurture me and share the dream with me. I count my blessings each day you are by my side."

As the crowd cheered loudly, both women appeared overcome with emotion. Looking out over the sea of faces, Louise paused to collect herself.

"My vision for the future is for OWL's Haven to be one of many lesbian retirement villages in this country. Before another ten years have passed, I want to see what we have achieved here replicated for our older community members in all states. We need to ensure that the private care industry caters to the whole of our LGBT community, so that there is a welcoming home for all of us and so that no couple ever needs to be separated, especially at a time when they need each other the most."

Renewed cheering greeted this statement, with many women standing in ovation. Graciously acknowledging the response, Louise laughed.

"And now, I'm told that lunch is being served in the main marquee. Again, thank you so much for coming and for your continued support. Enjoy the rest of the day."

The crowd clapped and cheered as Louise and Caro stepped down from the stage and were immediately surrounded by friends and well-wishers.

Jenna sighed. "What a beautiful speech. She's an amazing woman, isn't she? Even if she did have all that money, starting OWL's was still an enormous risk."

Leslie finished her glass of champagne. "Well, I for one am delighted she did, because heaven knows where I would be now if this place wasn't here."

"Or any of us, for that matter," Daphne added, putting her arm around Sparrow.

"Well here's a table of miscreants, if ever I saw one," Louise announced with a smile as she walked up. "Do you mind if I sit with you for a moment?"

Meg moved her chair over to give Louise more room. "We were just saying what a great speech you gave."

Louise smiled. "The public relations company wanted a big song and dance with speeches from the mayor and all and sundry, but I put my foot down and said no. The chair of the board agreed that I'd be the only one to speak. We wanted to keep it as informal as possible."

Jenna hesitated. "Louise, you don't have to answer if you think this is too personal a question, but I'm curious. What triggered the dream that you referred to in your speech?"

Louise filled her glass, taking in the expectant faces of the women around the table. "It's not personal at all, I'm happy to tell you. I was working in a nursing home back in the late eighties. The patients were quite elderly and most had some sort of minor health issue. I had just arrived back at work from my holidays and had been assigned a new patient called Mary, who had recently been admitted by her family after a bad fall. I went in to introduce myself to her and she refused to acknowledge me. Over the weeks, no matter what we did, she wouldn't talk to anyone and refused to take part in any of the activities. She just sat, staring out of the window.

"One night I was working late, and as I passed her door, I thought I heard her crying. When I went in, she was visibly upset and clutching a photograph of a woman around about her own age. I sat on her bed and just held her while she cried. She eventually told me that the woman in the photo was her lover of over thirty years. They had been separated when Mary's family had forcibly admitted her to the nursing home. She had no idea where her lover was. She only knew that her brother's family had evicted her from the home that the two of them had shared for all that time. She was terribly distressed. The laws were different in those days and unfortunately, with Mary in care, her partner had no protection from her family members. I was so incredibly angry that these two women had been treated so badly that I promised I would do what I could to help."

"What a bloody despicable family. Were you able to do anything for her?" Leslie asked.

Louise smiled. "Well, not as much as I would have liked. However, my manager was also gay, so I took the problem to her. In the end, we found Sarah, Mary's partner, and managed to get them both admitted to the local retirement home. It wasn't the perfect solution, but it was the best we could manage. At least they were together, even if it meant keeping their love a secret. It was then that I decided that if I ever had the money, I would open a lesbian retirement village, so other women wouldn't have to go through that agony. I just wish OWL's was bigger. I hate having to turn women away."

Allie raised her glass. "Well, I would like to offer a toast to you and to all you have done. I am so incredibly grateful for OWL's. What you have provided for us is the most wonderful gift you could ever give and we will be forever grateful."

"Hear, hear," the rest of the table joined in.

Laughing, Louise bowed in acknowledgement. "Thank you so much, ladies. You have no idea how important it is to me that you're happy living here. Now, I had better keep circulating, so enjoy the rest of your day and I'll see you all soon."

"Wow, what a story," Jenna said quietly as she watched Louise walk away to greet more visitors.

"It makes you realise what a difference one person with passion can make," Allie mused.

"Well, I think it's time we ate," announced Meg, breaking the serious mood. "It looks like lunch is being served and if I don't eat something soon, this champagne is going to make me do something I will probably regret,"

"Best idea you have had all day, Meg," Leslie quipped. "Lead on to the feast."

The sound of singing floated across the grounds as the gay and lesbian choirs from Canberra, Sydney and Wollongong gave their finale; a rousing rendition of the eighties hit "Celebration". Most of the audience joined in the singing, with many people dancing on the grass.

"Hell, I remember when this first came out," Daphne recalled, gently twirling Sparrow around. "I must have danced to this hundreds of times."

"Kool and the Gang. They used to play it at Ruby's in Sydney all the time," Sparrow said. "God, it seems like a million years ago. I don't think I can even remember being that young anymore."

The song finished to wild applause as the choirs took their bow.

"Damn, I always hate it when they finish. They are so good I could listen to them for hours," Daphne said, catching her breath as the singers left the stage.

Sparrow took her hand. "They have CDs on sale. We could go over and buy one if you'd like to."

Daphne beamed in delight. "That sounds like a wonderful idea; a perfect souvenir to remind us of a wonderful day."

Meg and Allie sat quietly together in the garden. The last guest from the anniversary party had left, and many of the residents were making their way back to their homes. Allie leant her head against Meg's shoulder, watching the sun set over the lake.

"It was a great party," she said softly.

"I think Louise and Caro were happy with the way it went," Meg agreed. "I'm so glad Amy Tang and her family came. It was wonderful to have the chance to personally thank her for everything she's done for our community."

"It's been quite a year, hasn't it?" sighed Allie. "When you think of where we were twelve months ago and what has happened to us all since…" She shook her head. "If you'd told me we would go through all these changes in such a short space of time, I would never have believed it."

Meg turned, kissing the top of Allie's head. "I have to say, I love the two of us living together again."

"Well, at least now, I really can keep an eye on you."

"We might have to prod Daphne about asking Sparrow to move in with her," Meg mused. "If we leave it to her it'll never happen."

Allie shook her head. "Darling, I really think Sparrow is perfectly capable of taking matters into her own hands when she feels they're both ready."

"I suppose so. Who'd have thought that quiet, timid little Sparrow was so feisty and determined! I have to say, it is wonderful to see the effect she has had on Daphne. Of course, we still have Pat and Bella's wedding to come; the icing on the cake as it were."

Allie sat up, stretching, "I do love a wedding; all that pomp and ceremony. It's so romantic."

"Sometimes Allie, you are so traditional." Meg laughed. "I really don't think Bella is going to be in a white wedding dress complete with bridesmaids."

Allie slapped Meg's arm. "I know that, but it is a fairy tale all the same, isn't it?"

Meg put her arm around Allie's shoulder. "Yes, darling, it is. I couldn't be happier for them. If two people ever deserved something wonderful, it is those two."

Allie yawned. "Come on, you, why don't we go back home and make a fairy tale of our own?"

Meg rose from the bench.

"Only if I can be the big bad wolf," she grinned.

Chapter 35

AUTUMN

THE GARDEN BY THE LAKE at OWL's Haven looked spectacular. Both staff and residents had worked tirelessly over the past week to create the perfect setting for Bella and Pat's wedding. A large gazebo had been erected on the lawn, the supporting frame covered in soft white muslin. A jasmine covered trellis had been attached to each side and the scent of the cascading flowers carried on the gentle breeze. Draped over the roof, the muslin was tied off at each corner with rainbow ribbons. Twenty pots of red roses in full bloom created an aisle to the podium. Chairs were placed on either side of the rose aisle and these were rapidly filling with friends, family and residents.

Pat stood in front of the celebrant's podium with Daphne by her side. Peering at her watch, she began pacing back and forth in her small allotted area, constantly checking the entrance, until Daphne finally grabbed her hand and stilled her.

"Hey, just relax. She will be here, you know."

Pat sighed, rubbing her hands on her pants. "I know. I just don't want anything to go wrong,"

Daphne studied her. After much consultation, Pat had decided on black silk pants, shirt and jacket, with a rainbow coloured vest and bow tie. As Best Woman, Daphne worse a matching vest, with an open necked shirt and no jacket. Seeing Daphne watching her, Pat frowned.

"What's wrong? Is my tie crooked?" she asked, bringing her hand to her throat.

Daphne laughed, "No, of course not. I was just thinking how handsome you look in that outfit. It fits you perfectly."

"Oh, right, thanks." Casting another worried look towards the entrance, Pat turned suddenly to Daphne "You've got the ring, haven't you?"

"It's here, right where you watched me put it half an hour ago," she answered calmly, patting her vest pocket.

"And my tie's straight?"

"Yes, mate, your tie's straight, but I think that Bella would marry you even if it was crooked."

"Yes, I know, but…"

"I know," Daphne repeated gently, "you don't want anything to go wrong."

A flash of panic crossed Pat's face. "What if I forget my vows?"

Daphne gave Pat an affectionate look, placing a hand on her arm. "Do you honestly think you are going to forget how much you love Bella? Just remember all the love you feel and the words will come to you."

Pat nodded. "I know, it's just…I can't believe we're finally doing this. The two of us have dreamt about this day for so long. We'd even discussed going to New Zealand to get married. Then Bella's cancer came and we both pushed away the dream, frightened that it would be tempting fate to even talk about it. Now I'm standing here thinking it's all a fantasy and I'm going to wake up to just another ordinary day." Pat blew out a big breath. "It's crazy, isn't it? Nothing's really going to be different and yet it feels like my whole life is changing." Running her hand through her short hair, she looked sheepishly at Daphne. "Hell, I'm glad you're here. I'd be a total basket case without you."

Daphne laughed quietly. "You mean as opposed to the semi basket case that you currently are?" Leaning in close, she put her hand on Pat's arm. "And just for the record, it's not crazy. You and Bella deserve this happiness. It's the culmination of everything you've been through, the pot of gold at the end of your rainbow."

Pat cleared her throat, her fragile emotions threatening to overwhelm her. Gazing up, she scanned the sky. "It looks like that predicted shower is going to hold off as well."

The weather had been an unknown factor in the planning; March in Berry was sometimes unpredictable. Bella and Pat had both wanted an outdoor wedding by the lake, but an alternative indoor setting had been planned just in case the weather didn't cooperate. However, the day had dawned clear and bright with a slight breeze, prompting everyone to declare that it was a sign that God obviously approved of gay marriage.

Allie held Bella's hand as the chauffeured car carried them to the venue. When Bella had asked her several weeks ago to be *Matrona d'Onore*, or Matron of Honour, Allie had been incredibly touched.

"But don't I have to be married to be Matron of Honour?" Allie had asked.

Bella had waved her hand dismissively. "I want someone with me that I love, and apart from Pat, I can't think of anyone else that I would rather share this moment with."

"What are you thinking?" she asked Bella as the car made its way slowly to the lakeside venue.

Bella turned to Allie. "For so many years we had to hide our relationship, worried that we would be shunned, or worse. Now I am on my way to stand up in front of so many people and, out loud, declare my love for the woman who has been the source of all my love and joy for the past forty-five years. It all feels a bit..."

"Surreal?" prompted Allie.

Bella nodded. "*Sì*. Surreal, but so wonderful."

As the car drew to a halt, Allie leant over and placed a soft kiss on Bella's cheek.

"Well, I wish the two of you another lifetime of happiness."

The driver opened the car door, offering her hand to help Bella out. As Allie came around from the other side of the vehicle, she signalled for the music to start. Allie handed Bella the small posy of jasmine and carried out a last minute check of their outfits. Holding her arm out for Bella, she winked as her friend fell into step beside her.

"Are you ready to make Pat the happiest woman in the world?"

"You may have to stop me from running down the aisle," Bella said, laughing joyfully.

Pat turned to watch as Bella walked towards her. She had never seen Bella look more stunning. The russet gold silk suit she'd chosen set off her olive skin beautifully and Bella's smile radiated sheer joy as she drew closer to the podium. When she stood at Pat's side and took her arm in front of the celebrant, Pat's eyes filled with tears.

The celebrant stepped forward

"We are gathered here together…"

A hush fell over the crowd as Pat turned to face Bella, ready to make her vows. As the breeze lightly ruffled her hair, Pat gazed down into the eyes of the woman she had loved and admired for so many years. Her heart pounding, she took a deep breath and prayed her voice wouldn't fail her as she said the most important words of her life.

"I, Pat Maree Campbell, join with you, Bella Patricia Fiorisi to celebrate our marriage. I promise to always share the joys and the sorrows life gives us, with my hand and heart entwined in yours. I respect your strength, I honour your soul and I adore your passion. With this ring, I offer you all that I am, with love and the wish that I may spend the rest of my life in your heart."

Bella looked down at her hand as Pat gently slipped the ring onto her finger. Blinking back tears, she struggled to compose herself. Clasping Pat's hand tightly, she declared her vows.

"I, Bella Patricia Fiorisi, join with you, Pat Maree Campbell, to celebrate our marriage. With love, I promise to dance with you in times of joy, to comfort you in times of sadness and to always be your partner in all things. With this ring I ask you to continue to share a lifetime of love with me, for no matter what we may encounter together, our home is in each other's hearts."

As Bella placed the gold band on Pat's finger, she felt her trembling with emotion. Lovingly, she placed her hand against Pat's cheek, gently wiping away a single tear.

"*Cara, Ora siamo una cosa sola*, now we are one," she murmured softly.

The celebrant gestured to the couple, delight plain on her face. "And so as these two women have offered themselves to each other with love and respect, I announce, with enormous joy, that they are officially, legally and indisputably... married."

Pat bent to kiss Bella as the guests broke out in cheers and clapping. Camera shutters clicked and friends celebrated with hugs and laughter. As Pat turned to face their witnesses with Bella clasped in her arms, she found them both instantly surrounded by friends.

———— ⚜ ————

Meg made her way to Allie's side and took her hand, entwining their fingers. Quietly, they watched as Bella and Pat accepted everyone's congratulations.

"I just want to capture this moment and keep it in my heart forever," Allie murmured, drawing Meg closer.

"There is a sense of magic in the air, isn't there? I have to admit, I cried when they said their vows. Poor Pat was a nervous wreck before you and Bella arrived. I thought Daphne was going to have to give her a sedative."

Allie laughed. "If I hadn't seen Bella looking for her glasses that she had just put in her purse and heard her muttering to herself in Italian, I would have sworn that she was totally unruffled."

Together they followed the crowd to the lakeside edge, where the wedding photographer had already set up her camera.

Once the official photographs had been taken, Louise called for silence from the assembled guests. "Bella and Pat would like to invite you all to join them at their reception. Could you please make your way over to the reception marquee."

The guests entered the dining area, marvelling at the decorations. Snowy white tablecloths, small vases of flowers and votive candles graced each table. A larger table at the top end of the marquee held a huge wedding cake, while off to the side half a dozen bain-marie's held a mixture of hot and cold food.

Sparrow, Daphne, Caro and Louise hurried over to join Meg and Allie.

"A table for six then?" Allie queried.

"Sounds perfect," Sparrow agreed.

Linking arms, the six women set off to find a table.

⸻

An hour later as everyone was finishing their meal, Daphne got to her feet and tapped her glass with a spoon. As the room quietened, she nervously cleared her throat.

"Today I have been privileged to be a part of one of the happiest events that we have experienced at OWL's. Two of my closest friends have finally been able to have their relationship of forty-five years legally recognised. They can now be officially and truthfully acknowledged as an old married couple."

Waiting for the cheers and laughter to subside, Daphne winked at a beaming Pat.

"Those of us that know this wonderful couple know their story and have been lucky enough to share part of their journey with them. We have seen firsthand the love and devotion that these two women share, and we have all been recipients of their kindness and generosity. The other night I was reading a poem that was one of my favourites as a child, and with your permission, I would like to read it as a tribute to their lives together, both past and future. *The Owl and the Pussy Cat went to sea, in a beautiful pea green boat...*"

As Daphne read the poem, Caro turned to Louise to whisper, "It really doesn't get any better than this, does it?"

Louise's eyes filled with tears. "It's everything I dared to dream about all those years ago," she replied huskily. "I can't believe we all made it a reality."

"*And hand in hand, on the edge of the sand, they danced by the light of the moon, the moon, the moon. They danced by the light of the moon.*" Daphne raised her glass. "Friends, please join me in a toast. Pat and Bella."

Everyone in the marquee rose to their feet as one.

"Pat and Bella."

Epilogue

Six Weeks Later

THE SMALL CITROEN 2CV SPED through the French countryside. It was six in the morning, the early fog was starting to burn off and Meg watched as they passed fields full of well-fed sleepy cows. She smiled at Allie, who was studiously concentrating on navigating the narrow, twisting country road.

"I wish you would tell me where we're going," Meg said again. "At least give me some kind of a hint as to why we're up at this ungodly hour?"

"Nuh uh, I've told you, you'll see when we get there and not a moment before."

Meg sat back in her seat, pouting. Their decision to travel to Paris had been made just after Pat and Bella's wedding. Meg had secretly arranged for it to appear that the newlyweds had just "won" a trip to Italy for their honeymoon. She knew that they both wanted to go back one last time, but their finances wouldn't allow it. Pat had tried to remember filling out the winning form for the contest at the shopping centre, but was soon caught up in the excitement of planning the trip. Whilst she was organising the honeymoon, Meg had suggested to Allie that the two of them go back to Paris, 'just for old times' sake'.

The last two weeks with Allie had finally banished Meg's memories of her last stay in the city. Staying in a small flat in the 9th District, they spent their time together visiting galleries, antique shops and cafes. They stayed up till the early hours and slept late, wrapped in each other's arms. Two nights before they were due to leave for home, Allie had made an announcement at dinner.

"Oh, by the way, I've hired a car and we're spending the day in the country tomorrow."

Meg had looked up, surprised. "Oh, what a lovely idea. Anywhere in particular?"

Allie smirked. "You'll have to see when you get there."

Despite Meg's best efforts, Allie had steadfastly refused to tell her where they were going. Looking out the window, she noticed that the fields they had been driving through had given way to vineyards. Row upon row of vines stood like sentinels, their buds just starting to appear.

Allie slowed the car and turned into a small rutted lane. Curious, Meg peered around, but could still see nothing but grapevines.

"Where are we going?" she asked again, even more puzzled.

"Patience. Your questions will be answered just over the top of this hill."

Allie drove slowly up the lane, the small car managing the steep incline perfectly. Meg sat forward in her seat, excitement building as they neared their destination. When they reached the crest of the hill, she gasped in delight.

There, spread out a little ways below them, were three hot air balloons. Two were almost fully inflated, while the third one was still being prepared. Meg gazed in wonder at the spectacle of colours.

As she pulled into the makeshift parking area, Allie grinned at the stunned expression on Meg's face.

"Well, are you going to sit there all day or are we going hot air ballooning?" she asked, opening the car door.

Meg climbed out of the vehicle and threw herself into Allie's arms. "You remembered," she whispered.

Allie linked her arms around Meg, pulling her more tightly against her body. "Of course I remembered. It took a bit of organising because they don't usually fly over this region, but I do have some powers of persuasion too, you know."

They walked to the smaller balloon and the pilot took them through the safety briefing, by which time the balloon was ready for boarding. The pilot helped them into the basket and the two women settled into their positions next to each other. As the pilot prepared for take-off, Meg was delighted to realise that this flight was just for the two of them.

Slowly, the basket began to rise as their pilot opened the burners. As the ground fell away from under them, Meg trembled with excitement. Leaning on the basket's edge, she was entranced at the rows and rows of vines stretching out below them like a patchwork quilt. The fog had completely burnt off and the two other balloons provided glorious splashes of colour against the peerless blue sky above them.

"It is even more beautiful than I expected, a real dream come true," she murmured in wonder.

Allie handed her a glass of champagne and gently clinked their glasses together. "Well, I hope you know that I intend to spend the rest of my life trying to make your dreams come true." Looking out on the vista unfolding before the still rising balloon, she leant into Meg and whispered softly,

"After all these years, we really are now having the time of our lives."

Meg took Allie's hand. "As long as we are together, my darling, then I can't imagine wanting anything else."

About Jane Waterton

As a daughter of a bookseller, Jane's love of books was actively encouraged from a very early age. In her early twenties she wrote poetry and song lyrics, but at the age of 45, after a very funny lunch with friends, an idea germinated for her first full length novel.

Although originally from Sydney, Jane has for the past six years, lived and worked in a small remote town in the red desert region of Western Australia with her partner and fur family. Here she dreams of eventually retiring to the coast and writing full time.

CONNECT WITH JANE WATERTON:
Webseite: www.janewaterton.com.au
Facebook: www.facebook.com/jane.waterton

Other Books from Ylva Publishing

www.ylva-publishing.com

Cast Me Gently

Caren J. Werlinger

ISBN: 978-3-95533-391-1
Length: 353 pages (100,000 words)

Teresa and Ellie couldn't be more different. Teresa still lives at home with her Italian family, while Ellie has been on her own for years. When they meet and fall in love, their worlds clash. Ellie would love to be part of Teresa's family, but they both know that will never happen. Sooner or later, Teresa will have to choose between the two halves of her heart—Ellie or her family.

Getting Back

Cindy Rizzo

ISBN: 978-3-95533-395-9
Length: 239 pages (73,000 words)

At her 30th college reunion, Elizabeth must face Ruth, her first love who bowed to family pressure long ago. As they try to reconcile the past, Elizabeth must decide whether she is more distrustful of Ruth or of herself. Is she headed for another fall or does she want to be the one who walks away this time? It's not easy to know the difference between getting back together and getting back

Walking the Labyrinth

Lois Cloarec Hart

ISBN: 978-3-95533-052-1
Length: 267 pages (67,000 words)

Is there life after loss? Lee Glenn, co-owner of a private security company, didn't think so. Crushed by grief after the death of her wife, she uncharacteristically retreats from life. But love doesn't give up easily.

All the Little Moments

G Benson

ISBN: 978-3-95533-341-6
Length: 350 pages (132,000 words)

Anna is focused on her career as an anaesthetist. When a tragic accident leaves her responsible for her young niece and nephew, her life changes abruptly. Completely overwhelmed, Anna barely has time to brush her teeth in the morning let alone date a woman. But then she collides with a long-legged stranger…

Coming from Ylva
Publishing

www.ylva-publishing.com

Rewriting the Ending

hp tune

A chance meeting in an airport lounge and a shared flight itinerary leaves Juliet and Mia connected. But how do you stay connected when you've only known each other for twenty four hours, are destined for different continents and each have a past to reconcile?

Welcome to the Wallops

Gill McKnight

Jane Swallow has always struggled to keep peace, friendship, and equanimity within the community she loves, but this year everything is wrong. Her father has just been released from prison and is on his way to Lesser Wallop with the rest of her travelling family. Her job is on the line, and her ex-girlfriend has just moved in next door. Only a miracle can save her.

Quoted in Chapter 35

"The Owl and the Pussycat" by Edward Lear, Nonsense Songs, Stories, Botany, and Alphabet, 1871